ALL GOD'S CHILDREN

ALL GOD'S CHILDREN

A NOVEL BY

ARTHUR LYONS

 MASON/CHARTER   NEW YORK

For Andora
whose love has
sustained me.

ALL GOD'S CHILDREN

CHAPTER ONE

Maybe it was one of those days when you don't want to get out of bed because something is waiting for you.

Or maybe it was one of those days when you don't want to get out of bed because nothing is waiting for you, and that's worse.

Or maybe it's just knowing that the telephone book beside your bed is full of names that have been dead for half a lifetime and others that shouldn't be living at all.

Or maybe it's the sky beyond the windows where it looks like rain, but the rain never falls.

But finally you do manage to get up and shower the ghost and shave the spirit and go out and drive ninety miles an hour to make yourself feel brave—a plastic value, as they say—and then slow it down to forty and wonder if that's the coward.

All that being true or untrue, I did get up that morning and went out under a sky that refused to rain and drove off at a cowardly forty through gray city streets where other people were just getting out of bed beside similar phone books of the buried or about-to-die. I was on my way to see a man about a job.

The house was in Olympian Estates, one of the new, expensive, ivy-covered developments that were rapidly scaling the wild and weedy sides of Benedict Canyon. It was long and flat-roofed and one-storied, two parts white brick to one part smoked glass. Across the front, cypress trees sprouted like gigantic asparagus spears. Lining the circular asphalt driveway, white, Doric columns alternated with pedestaled statues of fig-leafed Greek gods.

I made a U-turn and parked in front of the house and went past the statues up the stone steps to the front door. The man who answered the door was not old but too old by quite a few years for the tightfitting, flared slacks and knit body shirt he was

1

wearing. He was big, looking as if at one time he might have been athletic, but now the weight hung loose on his large frame and was sliding steadily down toward his midsection. What little hair he had was dark brown and self-consciously spread over his skull like a thin layer of butter, to cover as much scalp as possible. His face was jowly and well seamed, and his brown eyes were small, closely set, and heavily bagged. Right then, the eyes seemed to be dulled by despair—and, from what I could smell, Scotch.

"Yes?" he asked in a voice that sounded faintly annoyed.

"Mr. Haynes?"

"Yes?"

"I'm Jacob Asch."

"Oh, right," he said, grabbing my hand and pumping it vigorously. "Thanks for coming up. I appreciate it. Come in."

He stood back and I went inside. He closed the door and I followed him into a large, high-ceilinged living room that had beige grasscloth walls, a large stone fireplace, and thick carpeting the color of lemon sherbet. Two of the walls were glass, beyond which was a large swimming pool surrounded by more Greek gods. On the far side of the swimming pool the sides of the canyon dropped away sharply and the gray floor of the city spread out and merged with the steel-gray sky.

"Miserable goddamn weather," he said, motioning toward the pool. "What is it now—the third day of this? If it would only rain, or something, and get it over with."

He sounded irritated. I guessed the irritation had to do with things other than the weather.

"It's supposed to clear up by tonight," I said. "Or so the weather report says."

"Weather report!" he snorted. "What the hell do they know? They tell you it's going to rain when it's 110 out. They tell you it's going to be sunny and it rains—"

He caught himself as if sensing how ridiculous his tirade was and motioned to a low-slung couch by the fireplace. "Sit down."

I was about to, when a woman came into the room. She was dressed in a silk nightgown over which she wore a powder-blue, terrycloth bathrobe tightly sashed at the waist. She was thin and pale, and her long, black hair was liberally streaked with gray. Her features were sharp and harsh but not totally unpleasant, like erosional remnants standing out on some desert landscape.

She managed a weak smile and came over to me, holding out a thin, pale hand.

"I'm Cynthia Haynes," she said without waiting for her husband to introduce us. "You must be the detective. Robert told me he'd called you."

She said it as if she were trying to dissociate herself from the act. I looked over at Robert Haynes who looked less than pleased with his wife's appearance. "You shouldn't be up, dear," he said, and then to me: "Cynthia has been in bed with a nasty cold for the past week. This is the first time she's been up and around."

Cynthia smiled faintly. "I feel much better today. You will have to forgive my appearance, Mr.—"

"Asch."

"Asch," she repeated. "Do sit down."

I sat down on the couch, and she sat in one of the chairs facing me. "I think I will have some tea," she said. "May I offer you something, Mr. Asch? Coffee, perhaps?"

"No, thanks."

She turned toward a door which I assumed led to the kitchen and shouted: "Maria!"

The door opened and a rotund Mexican woman in a shiny pink maid's uniform stuck her head through.

"Maria, I would like some tea with lemon, please."

The woman nodded and disappeared.

"Maybe I'll fix myself a drink before we get started," Robert Haynes said, still standing. "Would you like one?"

"No, thanks."

He went over to the bar on the far side of the room, poured himself a double Scotch on the rocks, and rejoined us, sitting on the opposite end of the couch.

"You said on the phone that your daughter is missing."

"That's right," he said, and then added quickly: "Susan is my wife's daughter. She is my stepdaughter."

"How long has she been missing?"

"This time," he said, "six days."

"What do you mean by 'this time'?"

"She ran away from home at the beginning of summer, right before school let out. She was supposed to have graduated from high school in June, but she ran off before her finals. We had no

3

idea where she had gone until last month, when I started getting gas charges she'd signed on one of my credit cards. Susan had her own car, and I'd given her duplicates of several of my credit cards. Anyway, I had the license numbers on the charges traced and found out they belonged to trucks registered to some Jesus commune out near Fillmore called the Word of God. After doing some more checking, I found out she'd been living at the commune for the past two months. My credit cards and the car we'd bought her—a brand-new Mustang—had become community property."

He frowned and took a swallow of his drink.

"Where did she meet these people?"

"I don't know. Probably on the street. They're all over Hollywood Boulevard, passing out their damn leaflets. Here, I'll show you."

He put his drink down on the coffee table and left the room. While he was gone, Mrs. Haynes and I sat smiling rather lamely at each other. Robert came back with a folded handout, about four inches by seven, which he gave me.

Printed across the top of the paper in bold type was THE WORD OF GOD, and beneath that was a quote from the Book of Revelations: "And he is clothed in a garment sprinkled with blood, and his name is called the Word of God. And the armies of heaven, clothed in fine linen, white and pure, were following him on white horses." The rest of it was the standard, morbid, doomsday tripe spiced up with quotes from the Bible, and a mercifully short "I-was-once-a-sinner-too" revival-meeting testimonial by the group's founder, a man named Aaron Sievers whom I assumed was the one the armies of heaven were supposed to be following on white horses. I skimmed through the text to the end, where there was an address and a phone number for inspired sinners to call and get saved.

"Mind if I keep this?" I asked.

"No, take it."

I folded it and put it in my pocket. "You said Susan has been missing for six days. She came back, I take it."

"We had her brought home," Haynes said, "for her own good."

"What do you mean, you 'had her *brought* home'?"

"Just what I said. Have you ever heard of Larry Farnsworth?" I said I hadn't.

4

"He used to be a private detective," he said, as if it were scoring points with me. "Then his own son was cornered on the street by some fanatical Jesus group and got brainwashed. He saw the kind of psychological damage groups like that can do to kids. Now he specializes in helping other people get their children back from outfits like the Word of God. He got Susie back for us."

"How?"

"The only way possible. He went out to the commune with me, and we threw her into the car and got her the hell out of there."

"How old is Susan?"

"She was eighteen in July."

"Then she's a legal adult. What you're talking about is kidnaping, Mr. Haynes."

He made an abrupt, chopping motion in the air with his hand. "Technically, maybe, but not morally. Look, Asch, the kids in these communes are being brainwashed by these religious gangsters. They're actually taught to hate their parents. You should have seen Susie after we brought her out of that place. She refused to acknowledge that she knew either me or her mother. She kept saying she had no earthly parents, that she was born of the flesh and blood of Christ or some goddamn crap like that. She wouldn't even answer to her own name. She kept saying that her name was Sister Sarah."

"Why did she say that?"

"That was the name they gave her in the commune. They all get baptized with new names when they join the group."

"So what happened after you brought her back?"

"Farnsworth has a course he runs the kids through. He calls it 'deprogramming,' because he says their minds have been programmed like computers by these commune leaders, to respond automatically when you ask them certain questions. Farnsworth holds the kids in isolation and grills them about what they've been told about the Bible and their beliefs, until they break. He makes them face the possibility that all the garbage they've been fed maybe didn't come directly from God, and once they do that, the hold is broken."

"So what happened?"

"I don't know," he said. "Farnsworth claims the deprogramming was successful. Susie seemed fine when we got her home. Then a couple of days later she ran away again."

"Have you checked to see if she went back to the commune?"

"Farnsworth did. He says she didn't. He's keeping an eye on the place, though, just in case."

"Where was this 'deprogramming' done?" I asked.

"At a motel in Reseda called the Rainbow Lodge. Farnsworth always does it out there. He says it's isolated, and he can keep an eye on the kids better."

"How long did it take him to deprogram Susan?"

"Five days."

"How much did he charge you to do it?"

"A thousand."

"Did he give you a money-back guarantee?"

"*That* man?" Mrs. Haynes snorted.

I turned to her and said: "You don't sound as if you approve of Mr. Farnsworth."

"I don't," she replied sharply. "I was against hiring him in the first place. He is a shiftless, opportunistic golddigger, a scavenger living off other people's misfortune."

The look in her eye told me what she thought of me: one shiftless, opportunistic golddigger taking over where another shiftless, opportunistic golddigger had left off. I felt like telling her that I could think of easier ways to dig gold but didn't.

I turned back to Robert Haynes. "Have you met the leader of this commune? This Aaron Sievers character?"

"I met him when I went up there to get back Susie's Mustang."

"What's his story?"

"He's a con man, that's all. He knows an easy touch when he sees it. He's taking in a fortune with that religious racket of his. When those kids join that commune, they have to give up everything they own to the group. Some of them even give up things they don't own."

"How about the car? Did you get it back?"

"Yes, after I threatened to swear out a complaint on him for car theft. Luckily the car was registered to Cynthia and me, and Susie couldn't give it away. She didn't have the certificate of ownership."

"Where's the car now?"

"Locked up in the garage."

6

"Then Susie didn't take it when she ran away six days ago?"

"No."

I rubbed a hand over my chin and found a spot I had missed shaving. "I'm not exactly clear on what it is you want me to do, Mr. Haynes. Susan is legally an adult now. If she doesn't want to come home, there's very little I can do about it. I'm not going to get involved in any kidnaping scheme to bring her home against her will."

He held up his hands in protest. "No, no. We don't want you to get involved in anything like that. All we want you to do is find out where she is. Cynthia and I are both worried about her. We're afraid that in the frame of mind she was in when she ran away, she might get into some kind of trouble."

"Why? What frame of mind was she in?"

He grimaced and said: "Unbalanced."

"You mean psychologically?"

"Susan is a very emotional young girl," Cynthia said, heading off the question.

"What kind of trouble are you afraid she'll get herself into?" I asked anyone who cared to answer.

Mrs. Haynes said: "Susan has had a tendency in the past to pick up, well, rather unsavory companions."

"Unsavory, hell," Robert broke in. "They're trash."

"It seems to be a flaw in her character," the woman went on, throwing an irritated glance at her husband. Then she smiled a small, tight smile and said: "Sometimes I think it's a hereditary trait."

I wondered from which side of the family she might have inherited it, but I let the question die silently in my mind.

Cynthia Haynes turned suddenly toward the kitchen door and yelled: "Maria! Where *is* that woman? She's been getting impossible lately, absolutely impossible. If this keeps up, Robert, we are going to have to let her go."

The kitchen door opened then and Maria backed slowly through, carrying a tray. She came around the end of the couch, put the tray down on the coffee table, and straightened up with a grunt. "Es todo?"

"Yes, that's all," she said sharply. The woman waddled back around the couch and out of the room.

She poured herself a cup of tea from a small china teapot and squeezed in the juice from a quartered lemon. "Has Susan been in trouble before?" She took a sip of tea and leaned back in her chair, holding the cup and saucer just below her chin. "She's always been a problem child, but in the last three years she has gotten completely out of hand."

"How?"

"When she was little I used to have problems with her running away from home, but those were just childish pranks to get attention. It was when she turned fifteen that she started to become unmanageable. Her grades started falling off drastically, and then she started getting into trouble with the police. She ran away and hitchhiked all the way up to Seattle by herself before she was picked up for shoplifting and sent home. The next year she was caught joyriding with some delinquents in a car they had stolen from one of their parents. It cost me a fortune in lawyer's fees to get her out of that one without having it go on her record. Then, about a year and a half ago, she was arrested for possession of marijuana, along with a gang of motorcycle hoodlums. I saw them in court—filthy animals with tattoos all over their bodies."

It seemed to me that Cynthia Haynes took a little too much relish in recounting her daughter's infamous exploits. The more I heard, the more I felt myself beginning to sympathize with Susan. "What happened?"

"She was put on probation for a year, on the condition that she spend fourteen months in a special probation camp for girls."

"How was she after that?"

"She seemed to be fine. That was why we were so shocked when she ran away in June. We weren't expecting it."

"Do you remember the name of Susan's probation officer?"

"No, I'm afraid not."

"Lippmann, I think it was," Robert chimed in.

I took out my notebook and jotted down the name, scribbling the notation "Juvenile P.O." beside it. "Is she off probation now?"

"Yes," he said. "She got off in May."

"Do either of you have any idea why she would run away repeatedly like this?"

"Are you implying that we've been inadequate parents?" Mrs. Haynes said, leaning forward.

"No, I'm not. I was just wondering whether there was any sort of conflict in the home that—"

8

"I don't see what that could possibly have to do with finding her."

"At this stage I don't know what might help me find her, Mrs. Haynes. I'm just trying to gather some background information to work from."

She took a sip of tea and put the cup and saucer down on the table. "My daughter's problem is the same problem afflicting all children today. They have no sense of responsibility. You give them a little freedom and they interpret it as a go-ahead to run wild."

I thought it would be best to drop that line of questioning. "Do you know of anybody Susan might have contacted for help? If she needed a place to spend the night, maybe, or something like that?"

"No."

"How about friends? Did she have any?"

"Up until last year, she was best friends with a girl named Shelley Silverman. But the Silvermans would have let me know if Susan had showed up there."

I nodded. "You said up until last year, she and the Silverman girl were best friends. What happened to change things?"

"I wouldn't know."

"Do you have the Silvermans' phone number?"

"We have it somewhere. Robert can give it to you."

"What about boyfriends? Was Susan dating anybody steadily?"

"No," Robert Haynes said. "She was never serious about anyone, if that's what you mean."

"That's what I mean. Did she date much at all?"

He took a pull from his drink and watched us. "She went out a lot, yes."

"Would you happen to know the names of any boys she was dating?"

"Susan never discussed her dates with us," Cynthia said.

I wondered what they *had* discussed with Susan. "What about your former husband, Mrs. Haynes?"

She raised a hand to her throat and held it there. "What about him?"

"Do you think she might have gotten in touch with him?"

"No."

9

There was something in the certainty of her answer that bothered me. "How can you be so sure?"

"Because Susan hated Eric with a passion. They never got along—"

"That's not true," Robert broke in. "Susan always thought of Eric as her father even though he and Cynthia were divorced when Susan was just a baby. She never really accepted me as her father, even though I legally adopted her. She always went by the name of Gurney instead of Haynes."

Cynthia turned white around the mouth and glared at him lividly, but he either didn't notice or pretended not to. He went on: "When she was a kid, she used to run away and go to Eric's. He'd call, and then we'd have to go over and pick her up."

"How old was she then?"

"Uh, up to the time she was ten or eleven. I don't remember exactly. She stopped going over there a year or two after Cynthia and I were married. Yeah, I guess she was about eleven. But she still used that goddamn Gurney name."

There was a strange bitterness in his voice. He must have caught the sound of it, too, because he looked away from me quickly. His eyes met Cynthia's in a steady, angry glare. The tension growing between them seemed almost tangible, like a string being pulled tight from both ends. I stepped in and cut the string. "Have you checked with Eric to find out if he's seen her?"

"I talked to him a couple of days ago. He says he hasn't."

"Do you believe him?"

Haynes stood up and looked down at me. "I don't know why he would lie about it."

He went to the bar with the overcautious gait of a veteran alcoholic and took two ice cubes from the bucket on the counter and dropped them into his glass. I watched him pour a double shot of Chivas Regal.

"I'd like to talk to Gurney," I said. "Do you have his phone number?"

"No," his wife broke in suddenly.

I turned to her. "Why not?"

"Eric has taken no interest in Susan's welfare for fourteen years. There's no reason for him to get involved now. He'd only spread malicious lies."

"What kind of lies?"

10

"Never mind. I don't intend to discuss it. And I don't want that man brought into this. I want that clear. You will not talk to him."

"Look, Mrs. Haynes," I said. "Your husband called me here to try to find your daughter. If you want me to find her, okay. I can try. If you don't want me to find her, that's okay, too. But if you want me to find her, don't tie me up with all kinds of conditions and qualifications."

She tilted her head back slightly, sighting me down the length of her bony nose, and said: "I think we had better get one thing straight, Mr. Asch. It is *my* money that is paying your fee, not my husband's. And if you want this job, you will obey *my* conditions."

I wanted the job—no, that wasn't exactly true—I *needed* the job. I hadn't had a client in over a month, and the last one I did have had beaten me out of half of what he owed me. I was down to my last hundred and fifty in the bank. But I didn't need the money *that* badly.

I stood up. "Nice to have met you, Mrs. Haynes. I hope you find your daughter."

Robert Haynes put his drink down and followed me into the hall. He took hold of my sleeve just as I reached the front door. "Wait, Asch," he whispered, "don't leave."

"I came up here on your say-so, Haynes," making no effort to lower my voice. "You want to give me gas money or should I go back in there and ask your wife for it?"

He looked over his shoulder as if expecting the Furies to come sweeping down on him any minute and hustled me out the front door. "Listen, Asch," he said after we were outside: "Cynthia was against hiring a detective in the first place. I had to talk her into it—"

"I know. 'We're all scavengers living off other people's misfortune.' Well, I'm sure you can find somebody more to her liking. There are a lot of detectives in the city who would be glad to take her money and her orders. I can give you some names if you'd like."

He held up his hands. "Don't go off half-cocked. She just gets a little irrational when it comes to Eric."

"No kidding? I'd never have known. What's the deal with her, anyway?"

"Eric walked out on her, and she's never gotten over it. Then that phone call didn't help things any."

"What phone call?"

"When Eric found out about Susan being deprogrammed, he got hot. He doesn't think we should have hired Farnsworth. Said we should have left her in the commune. He called up Cynthia, and they got into a big row about it. As a matter of fact, that's what brought on this last attack."

"How did he find out about the deprogramming in the first place?"

He looked down at his feet. "It was my fault. I let it out when I called him."

"Whatever your wife's hangups are about her ex-husband, Haynes, I'm still not going to take on this case blindfolded and handcuffed—"

"Look, I'll give you Eric's phone number if you think it's important. Just don't let Cynthia know you've seen him. Pretend to humor her, and everything will work out fine; believe me."

"Is that how you've gotten along with her all these years?"

His gaze skirted mine, and he opened his mouth to say something, but nothing came out.

"I get a hundred and twenty a day plus expenses," I said, waiting for him to say it was too much, so I could walk. "Plus fifteen cents a mile."

"I'll see that you get it. Don't worry."

"And I'll want a retainer. Five hundred."

"I'll make out a check before you leave."

I felt another emotion moving in to replace my distaste for Cynthia Haynes—greed. I went back inside with him.

"Mr. Asch has agreed to stay on the job," he announced as we entered the room. "On your terms."

A small, confident smile crossed her lips, and she shifted in her chair. "If I find out you've gone against my wishes and talked to Eric, I will dismiss you immediately. You understand that?"

"I'd like to see Susan's room," I said.

"You show him to the room, dear," she said, looking pleased with her victory. She brushed her forehead weakly with the back of her hand and stood up. "I'm tired. I think I'll go to bed and rest. You can take care of the financial details. I'm sure Mr. Asch will want some expense money."

She turned away and then turned back. "Oh, and tell Maria that I would like some more tea. In my room."

She left without saying good-bye.

He watched her go and then turned to me. "Okay, come on. I'll show you Susan's room."

"You'd better tell Maria about the tea, first. We wouldn't want your wife to get upset."

"To hell with her," he said, then thought better of it and went out to the kitchen.

CHAPTER TWO

Susan's bedroom had its own sliding glass door out to the back yard. The heavy gray morning light poured in through the door, washing out the colors of the promotional posters of Led Zeppelin, Leon Russell, Carly Simon, and other, more obscure, rock performers that were plastered all over the walls.

The room was a good size, but the amount of furniture that was packed into it made it look smaller than it was. There was a queen-size bed flanked by two bedside tables and reading lamps, a bulky teakwood dresser, a writing desk, and a portable stereo set with dual speakers mounted on a movable console. Stacked casually on the shelves underneath the stereo were albums by the rock groups on the walls. The one on the top of the stack was by the Stones, its cover a close-up crotch shot of a pair of blue jeans.

I opened the door to the walk-in closet and started sorting through the clothes. There was enough there to sort through, though most of the outfits were for casual wear. I went through pockets whenever I found any but came up with nothing. I closed the door.

Haynes stood watching me from the doorway. The Scotch was starting to overtake him now, and he was swaying slightly as if moved by a firm but invisible breeze.

"Do you know what she took with her in the way of clothes?" I asked. "What she might be wearing?"

He blinked, and his eyes came into focus. "Huh? Uh, no. I don't know what she was wearing."

"How about an address and phone number for this Shelley Silverman you were supposed to get me?"

"Hmm?"

"Shelley Silverman."

"Oh yeah. Right. I'll see if I can find it."

"And while you're at it, see if you can find a picture of Susan. A recent one, if you've got it."

"I've got her graduation picture. It was taken last spring."

He left the room, and I started on the clothes in the dresser. I came up with a zero there, too, but I had better luck with the desk. Flipping through the pages of an unused school notebook, I came across a clean piece of white paper, neatly folded and tucked away between the pages. I opened it up and found it was a note, written in pencil, in an almost illegible scrawl. There was no date.

Dear Sue:

I'll be geting out of the slams pretty soon, just too more weeks. Six months is a long time. All I've thot about was you in here. I lie here after the lites are out and think about all the good times we had. Wheel have more good times, tho. We can split this town and go somewhere where nobody can hassel us, right?

I herd from Hank. He sends his love. He's got another three months to do on account of his violating parole. I really miss you Sue, like I never missed anybody before and that's the truth.

Gypsy.

I finished reading the letter as Haynes came into the room, holding an 8 x 10 color photograph. He handed it to me, along with a piece of paper with writing on it.

"There's the Silvermans' phone number and address. Eric Gurney's home number is on there, too."

I put the paper in my pocket. He eyed the letter in my hand with curiosity. "What's that?"

"It's a letter to your stepdaughter from somebody named Gypsy. You remember Susan ever mentioning anybody by that name?"

"Gypsy? No. I didn't know she had any girl friends besides Shelley."

"Gypsy isn't a girl."

"Not a girl?" he said with some surprise. "That's a funny name for a boy, isn't it?"

"It's probably a nickname."

"Well, who is he? What does it say?"

"That he wants to run away with her when he gets out of jail."

"Jail?"

"That's what it sounds like."

I handed him the letter. While he read it, I studied the picture. The girl was cute, but I wouldn't have called her pretty. She had large, green eyes and a round face with dimples on both cheeks that had been only partially wiped out by the photographer's touch-up job. Frizzy blond hair stood out from her head like an electrified halo.

"You don't have anything smaller than this?"

He wasn't listening. He was staring at the letter, his face chalky, his lips tightly pursed. I took it out of his hands, folded it up, and slipped it into my pocket with the phone numbers. "You don't have anything smaller than this?" I asked again, waving the picture in his face.

"Huh? No. Nothing recent, anyway." Reading the letter seemed to have sobered him up a little. His eyes grew hard as he stared at my pocket. "What are you going to do with that letter?"

"Try to find out who this Gypsy character is, for starters. Who was Susan's attorney for her probation trial?"

"Tom Hapke. Why?"

"How well do you know him?"

"He's been Cynthia's attorney since before we were married. Why?"

"I'd like to talk to him. You think you could call him and set up an appointment for me?"

"I suppose," he said. "What do you want to talk to him about?"

"Susan's case. If she was arrested and booked as a juvenile, there wouldn't be any record of it at the County Clerk's office. I could talk to her probation officer, but I doubt he'd give me the time of day. I haven't had very much luck with probation people."

"How is dredging up Susan's case going to accomplish anything? It's past history."

I patted my pocket. "This letter is from Susan's past, too. She obviously knew this Gypsy quite well, and he's obviously been in trouble with the law—"

"You think he was connected with her case in some way?"

"It's possible," I said.

16

He bit his lip and nodded thoughtfully. "When do you want to see Hapke?"

"This afternoon, if possible."

"I'll call," he said and moved self-consciously toward the door.

I followed him down the hall into a walnut-paneled den. He eased himself into the leather chair behind the desk, opened the address book beside the phone, found the number, and dialed it. He gave Hapke's secretary his name and then said, "Hello, Tom," almost immediately. I listened while he explained the situation to the attorney and asked if he could spare me a few minutes sometime that afternoon. Haynes said yes about four times, okay about three, then hung up.

"He says to come over at three. He'll see you then."

"Where is his office?"

"413 Roxbury, in Beverly Hills."

I got out my notebook and wrote it down. "Good. Your wife said you were going to take care of the financial arrangements—"

"Oh, yes," he said and got a checkbook out of the desk drawer. "What was it you said? Five hundred?"

"Right."

While he wrote out the check, I said: "I'd also like to talk to this Farnsworth. Do you also have a number for him?"

He ripped the check out of the book, tearing one corner of it in the process, then opened one of the other drawers and began rummaging through it. He came up with another address book, smaller than the other one. "Larry Farnsworth. 357–9089."

"Is that an office number?"

"No, that's his answering service. I don't think he has an office. He came up here to the house to arrange everything. I've got a private, unlisted number for him, too, if you want that. He gave it to me in case I had to reach him in an emergency."

I told him to give it to me and he recited it from the book.

"How did you get hold of Farnsworth in the first place?" I asked.

"I read an article in the paper about him and what he was doing, and looked him up in the phone book. The answering service number was listed, so I got in touch with him through that."

Sure. Look in the Yellow Pages under Deprogramming. I put away my notebook and told him I'd be in touch with him in a couple of days and let him know what I had come up with.

He showed me to the door and stood on the front step, watching me as I went down to the car. He was still standing there, looking dejected, as I pulled away from the curb and drove down the hill.

CHAPTER THREE

I drove into Beverly Hills and cashed the check at Haynes' bank, using the pay phone there to call both of Farnsworth's numbers. I got a busy signal at the private line and his answering service on the second call. The girl on duty said that Mr. Farnsworth was not available and would I care to leave my name and number. I told her I would call back, and hung up.

The address I had for Shelley Silverman was in a residential section of Beverly Hills just a few blocks north of Santa Monica Boulevard. I decided to drive over unannounced.

The house was in the middle of the block on a cool, quiet street well-shaded by pepper trees. It was an expensive ranchhouse with a flagstone facade and a brown shingle roof. I parked and walked up the circular driveway that cut across the huge expanse of lawn sloping toward the front door and rang the bell.

The door was opened by an attractive woman whose tanned and lineless face seemed to be effortlessly resisting the advance to middle age. Her brown hair was frosted and cut in a youthful shag. She was wearing a plain, orange dress open at the throat and cut well above the knee. She gave me a smile that asked me what I was going to try to sell her—a vacuum cleaner or a set of the *World Book Encyclopedia?*—and said: "Yes?"

"Mrs. Silverman?"

"Yes."

"My name is Jacob Asch," I said, taking out one of my cards. She looked at it, then back at me, confused.

"I'm working for Mr. and Mrs. Robert Haynes. I guess you know that their daughter has run away from home."

"Yes. They called here about a week ago. I told them I hadn't seen Susie. Shel hasn't seen much of Susie in over a year."

"That's what I understand. The Hayneses have engaged me to

19

try to locate her. I was wondering if I might talk to your daughter for a minute. Is she home?"

"Uh, yes, she is," she said uncertainly.

"Would it be possible to talk to her?"

She looked at the card again as if hoping to see some advice printed there and finally said: "I suppose. Won't you come in and sit down?"

She showed me into a spacious living room tastefully furnished in Danish modern and lots of dark, rich wood. Over the fireplace was a large oil portrait of Mrs. Silverman, looking young, beautiful, and queenly, dressed in a low-cut evening dress and wearing a garish diamond necklace.

"That's a beautiful portrait."

She smiled self-consciously. "Thank you. My husband had it done. I want to take it down, but he insists on keeping it up. Myself, I think it's rather gauche. Excuse me, and I'll see if I can find Shel."

She left the room, and I sat down on one end of a long couch and waited. She had not been gone more than three or four minutes when she returned, followed by a tall, incredibly built young girl with bleached blond hair and a dark tan. The eyes of the girl were startlingly blue and set wide apart. She had a small, surly mouth that was turned down at the corners in a mock pout. She was wearing an abbreviated yellow halter top and a pair of white cutoffs, moving with a natural, fluid sway to her hips, obviously aware of her own youthful sensuality.

Dredging up my own ancient memories of high school, I couldn't remember ever graduating with anything that looked like that. Maybe it was something in the diet nowadays. Or maybe it was just that they bloomed quicker and died quicker. Drunk in the seventh grade, acid trips in the eighth, sex in the ninth—it was an accelerated, 90-mile-an-hour trip by a generation that was experimenting for real with things that had been, and still were, for most people in the realm of lurid fantasy.

"Shelley," her mother said, "this is Mr. Asch. He's a private detective working for Susie's mother and father, and he wants to ask you a few questions."

"Hi," Shelley said unenthusiastically, flopping down in a chair and brushing back a wisp of yellow-white hair that had fallen over one eye.

"Hi, Shelley," I said, smiling.

Mrs. Silverman remained, and Shelley looked over at her and said: "If you don't mind, Mom, I'd like to talk to the man alone. Okay?"

Mrs. Silverman didn't look too happy about it, but she complied with her daughter's request, saying that if we needed her for anything, she would be in the kitchen. Once she was out of the room, the girl's shoulders drooped and she seemed to relax a little. But only a little. She looked at me mistrustfully and asked: "Why are you looking for Susie?"

"Because her parents think she might be in some kind of trouble. They want me to find her before that happens."

"What kind of trouble could she be in?"

"I was hoping you could tell me."

She started to fidget with a loose thread that was dangling from the seam of her cutoffs. "I haven't seen Susie since before graduation. In June."

"Where was that?"

"In school."

"I hear you two used to be best friends."

She nodded.

"What happened?"

"Nothing happened. We just kind of drifted apart. She started hanging out with different people, and we just kind of, uh, stopped seeing each other, that's all."

"What kind of people was she hanging around with?"

Shelley shifted uncomfortably in her chair. "Hey, look, I don't want to cause any trouble for Susie. I mean, maybe we're not best friends anymore, but I still like her, and I don't want to make any trouble for her. Whoever she wants to hang around with, that's okay by me."

She looked away from me self-consciously as if catching the defensive sound of her protests.

"I'm not trying to make trouble for Susie," I assured her. "Really. As a matter of fact, that's why I'm trying to find her—to head off any that might be coming her way."

"She *has* been getting herself into things the last couple of years."

"Is that why you parted company?"

21

"That was one of the reasons," she said. "Hey, have you got a cigarette?"

"I don't smoke."

"Bummer," she muttered, frowning, then stood up. "I've just *got* to have a cigarette. Excuse me a sec. I'll be right back."

I watched her leave the room, the weight shifting effortlessly and smoothly between those two rounded buttocks. Then I was alone under the watchful eyes of Mrs. Silverman in the portrait, which stared at me, chastising me for my wicked thoughts.

Shelley came back in with a lighted cigarette and a package of Winstons in her hand. She flopped back down in the chair, put the pack on the table beside her, and pulled an ashtray toward her.

"How long have you known Susie?"

"We've gone to school together since the sixth grade. But we only became close in high school."

"What kind of a girl is she?"

She smiled vaguely. "On the outside or on the inside?"

"There was a difference?"

"Yeah, there was. Susie's like two different people."

"How so?"

She wrinkled her forehead and said: "On the outside, she was hard and cold. But that was just a put-on. She was really supersensitive inside, although she'd never let anybody see it in a million years. She had a lot of trouble relating to people. She didn't trust anybody. Sometimes I got the feeling she didn't even trust me, and I knew her better than anybody."

"Why was she like that, do you think?"

She took a drag on her cigarette and exhaled. "She had a really big inferiority complex. She felt like nobody cared about her, you know? If you didn't know her, you'd never guess that in a million years, because she always acted so indifferent, like she didn't care about anything or anybody, but she was just afraid to let her feelings show."

"When you say she felt like nobody cared for her, you mean her parents?"

"Yeah. I think they were a big cause of it. She took her parents' divorce pretty hard. It was always a sore spot with her."

"Did you two talk about her parents much?"

"Not a lot. Once in a while she'd talk about it, but not often."

"What did she say?"

"She was kind of bitter that her father didn't come and see her at all."

"She liked her father?"

Shelley nodded grudgingly. "She wanted to go live with him, but her mother wouldn't let her."

"She didn't like it at home?"

"No. She and her mother didn't get along at all. That was why she kept running away all the time. She was always talking about going away and living on her own somewhere."

"Did she ever mention where she'd like to go if she could?"

She flicked a lengthening ash into the ashtray and looked at me steadily. "It depended on the day. One day, she'd be talking about going to work up north somewhere, Oregon or Washington, and the next, she'd be talking about going to Europe and bumming around. Susie's future was kind of fuzzy in her own mind. She liked to dream about it, but I don't think she ever had any definite plan in her head about what she was going to do."

"Did she have any other close friends besides you?"

Shelley tilted her head back and shook it slightly. "Nobody. Like I said, she never got along with other people. My other friends never knew what I saw in her. But Susie was a real blast to be around sometimes. We had a lot of fun times together." She said it with a wistful tone, as if she wished the fun times would return but knew they never would.

"What about guys? Did she date much?"

"She dated quite a bit, I guess, but nobody in particular."

"Anybody you can think of that she would contact?"

She shook her head uneasily. I was starting to reach the point of diminishing returns, so I decided to press her a little to see what came up.

"So what kind of a crowd did Susie start hanging around with that caused you two to go your separate ways? Was it the bikers she got busted with?"

Shelley put her thumbnail between her teeth and winced. "She was getting kind of distant before she started riding with those guys, but that was what kind of cooled me off entirely."

"What was the name of the group?"

"The Satan's Warriors," she said, as if having the name in her mouth disgusted her. "They were from Santa Monica."

23

I took down the name. "How did she get involved with them?"

"I don't know exactly. A couple of them used to come around the school once in awhile. I think she met them there. She started going out with one of them pretty heavy."

"You remember his name?"

She hesitated and then said: "John—something. I don't remember his last name. She just called him Gypsy."

A sudden exhilaration went through me. "Was this Gypsy the one she got busted with?"

"He was one of them."

"What happened? How did they get busted?"

"Susie was out cruising with them, and the cops stopped them. They were carrying some dope on them, I guess. Susie claimed the cops planted the stuff, but I don't know. Those guys were pretty heavy dopers anyway."

"Did you ever meet this Gypsy?"

Shelley put out her cigarette and nodded, avoiding my eyes. "What was he like?"

"An animal," she spat. "They were all animals." She threw a surreptitious glance toward the kitchen, then leaned forward intently and lowered her voice. "Say, you're not going to tell any of this to my mother, are you?"

"No. Anything you say will be held in the strictest confidence."

"Good," she said, but there was still a residue of doubt in her voice. "Because I wouldn't want any of this to get back to her, but Susie fixed me up with one of them once, a guy by the name of Hank. She said we'd have fun, that there was going to be a party at the beach, and that I'd really like this Hank, that he was really a great guy with a great sense of humor. Some sense of humor. He got really smashed out of his mind on wine and reds and tried to rape me right there on the beach. I wound up walking home. I told Susie that after that, I didn't want to get fixed up with any more of her friends."

"What did Susie see in those guys if they were such animals?"

"I don't know," Shelley said, crinkling up her brows. "I think she was just tripping herself out. She romanticized the whole scene in her mind. It was like—I don't know—when she talked me into going to that party, she sat me down and gave me a whole big lecture about how the Warriors and the Angels and groups like that were really not what people thought they were, that they were misunderstood heroes or something. She said they were the last real outlaws left and that society had given them a bad name because they were free and did what they wanted to do without taking any guff from anybody. She really made them sound exciting. I half-believed her when I went to that party. But I found out different pretty quick. They're everything society says they are. Just a bunch of wild pigs."

She was staring straight ahead, her eyes focused on a point behind me, lost in her own thoughts.

"Was Susie taking drugs?"

Her eyes snapped shut and then opened on me, once more clouded with mistrust. "I wouldn't know," she said.

"Come on, Shelley, you must have some idea," I said. "You two were still bumming around together then."

She swept back a few strands of blond hair from her forehead. "I've seen her smoke some grass occasionally, but that's all I ever saw. She might have gotten into something heavier with those guys, I don't know."

"I'm not asking because I want to bust Susie or turn her over to the police or anything like that, Shelley, I want you to understand that. I'm just trying to determine what kind of a predicament she might be in, if any. Do you understand?"

She nodded weakly, and I put away my notebook. "I guess those are all the questions I have for now, Shelley. I want to thank you for talking to me. You've been a great help." I handed her a card and said: "If you hear anything from Susie or from anybody who's seen her, I'd appreciate it greatly if you'd give me a call."

She took the card and looked at it, then put it down on the table. When she looked up again, she looked worried. "I sure hope Susie's not with those bikers again. Is that where you think she is?"

"I have no reason to think so," I half-lied. "Good-bye, Shelley."

I went out to the kitchen to say good-bye to Mrs. Silverman and then back through the living room to the front door. I paused at the door to take a farewell look at that smooth, brown, muscular body and felt my pulse quicken and my mouth go dry. Then something in me sagged, and I turned and went out, feeling suddenly and irrevocably old.

A dirty old man at thirty-four.

CHAPTER FOUR

I drove back into Beverly Hills and pulled into a gas station on little Santa Monica and told the attendant to fill up the tank. While he was doing that, I used a pay phone to call the *Chronicle*.

An unfamiliar voice at Mike Sangster's extension told me he was out on assignment. So I had the receptionist put me through to Julia Messinger in the library. Julia was in. After going through the standard how-the-hell-are-you and how-have-you-beens and extracting from me a promise to take her out to lunch some future, nebulous noontime, she agreed to pull any articles she had in the morgue on the Word of God commune and leave them at the front desk for me.

I went back to the car and paid the attendant and filed the receipt in my "R. Haynes" section of the glove compartment. Then I drove down to Roxbury Drive to keep my appointment with Thomas Hapke.

Hapke turned out to be a small, bespectacled man who, besides being an attorney, was a mentholated-cough-drop addict. Against a background of lozenges clicking against his teeth, he filled me in on Susan's case.

It seemed that Susan had been out riding one night with some Satan's Warriors when they were pulled over by the Santa Monica police and rousted. A subsequent pocket search came up with about a lid of stash, a dozen or so reds, an Army-issue K-bar knife, and a .22-caliber handgun, of the Saturday-night variety. Susan had no identification at the time, but because she looked young, she was separated from the others and booked as a juvenile.

When I asked Hapke about a "John AKA Gypsy," he came up with a name. He said that during the pretrial phase of the judicial proceedings, the prosecutor in the case of the other defendants had come to him and offered to have all charges against

Susan dropped in exchange for her testimony against one of the others in a contributing to the delinquency of a minor charge. She had refused. The name of the defendant was John Lee Hunter whose gang name was "Gypsy."

I left Hapke sucking his lozenges and drove downtown to the criminal division of the County Clerk's office. I found Hunter's name in the index and had the clerk pull the file. The details of his arrest were exactly as Hapke had said. He had been booked on contributing, possession of dangerous drugs, and possession of marijuana, but he had only been convicted for possession, to which he had pleaded guilty. The other charges had been dropped along the way, apparently due to plea bargaining. He had been sentenced to six months in the county jail and three years' probation. Taking six months from the date of his trial, that meant he should have been released some time around the beginning of the summer.

I gave the clerk back the file and used a pay phone downstairs to call Adult Probation. I asked for the "Index" and was connected with an officious-sounding female clerk who took down Hunter's name and put me on hold. She clicked back on the line a minute later and told me that his probation officer was Richard Weiskopf. I thanked her, deposited another dime, and dialed Sheriff's Homicide. I asked for Sergeant Al Herrera and left my name.

"Jake, kid," Al's gravelly voice broke in, "what's up?"

"Nothing much, Al. What's new with you?"

"Just the same old shit. People killing people."

"Listen, Al, I need a favor—"

"What else? I spend more time working on your cases than I do my own."

"That's because you know mine have a chance of being solved."

"That's very funny. Ha ha. You're a funny man, did you know that? What do you need?"

"Whatever you can get on a John Lee Hunter. He runs with an outlaw biker club called the Satan's Warriors—or he used to. He's on probation right now on a possession charge. His P.O.'s name is Richard Weiskopf." I spelled the name for him.

"What exactly do you need? If it's not too much, I can probably get it over the phone on an O.T.I."

"His rap sheet, any addresses you can get for him, parents'

names and address, employment record—anything. Oh, and a description. I don't even know what the cat looks like."

"When do you need the stuff? I mean, you're not in any great rush, are you?"

"Tomorrow sometime?" I asked hopefully.

"Tomorrow's fine," he said. "It'll have to be in the afternoon, though. I'm going to be tied up all morning."

"What time?"

"Say around four? At Luigi's. We can have a drink and bullshit."

"Sounds good. I'll see you then. Thanks, Al. Bye." I hung up and went over to the county lot where I had parked my car and drove the six blocks to the offices of the *Chronicle*.

The articles were waiting for me when I got there; the girl at the desk handed them to me without batting an eye. I thanked her and drove the gray afternoon streets over to Hollywood, wishing it would hurry up and rain and get it over with.

CHAPTER FIVE

I did my homework at a coffee shop on Hollywood Boulevard, over a ground sirloin dinner that was dried-out and tasteless. The articles comprised a series that had appeared on three consecutive Sundays in the county section. One of them dealt exclusively with the Word of God's founder and spiritual leader, Aaron Sievers, and the other two covered the commune and its operation.

The son of a Brownsville, Texas preacher who had made a small fortune selling "holy tablecloths blessed by Jesus Himself" to the credulous listeners of his nightly radio show, Sievers had at an early age seen the "hypocrisy of religion" and turned away from God. When he was sixteen he ran away from home and went to Los Angeles, the City of Sin, where he picked up odd jobs and indulged himself in sensual delights. He worked as a busboy, a bartender, and finally as a used car salesman. It was while he was a salesman that he got his first message from God, telling him to "go out and preach the Word of the Lord or die."

The terrified Sievers went back to his apartment and threw out the girl who was living there with him, swore off booze and dope, and took to the streets, Bible in hand. He spent most of his time on Hollywood Boulevard and the Sunset Strip, preaching to the young transients and runaways who hung around the head shops and rock clubs. Pretty soon he had picked up enough converts to finance a coffeehouse on the Strip where he gave out free food to needy street people.

After operating the coffeehouse for about six months, Sievers received another message from God, telling him to take the souls he had reaped and go north where he was to buy some property and found a commune. The article did not make it clear whether God or Sievers made the decision to put the commune in Fillmore, but from those modest beginnings, within two years he had expanded the commune into a $15,000-a-month operation and had managed to buy up 50 acres of prime agricultural land in the Santa Paula valley.

One of the first converts was an ex-Green Beret corporal named Michael Michelmore who had just returned home from a stint in Vietnam. Michelmore heard Sievers preaching one day to a group of hippies on Hollywood Boulevard and immediately knew he was face to face with the Lord. He took on the name Brother Isaiah, joined the ranks of the saved, and soon became Sievers' (who was now known as Moses) closest advisor.

It was Michelmore, the article said, who was primarily responsible for organizing the group along military lines. Upon entering the fold, all new members, or "recruits," as they were called, traded their worldly possessions for a white shirt and a biblical name and were assigned to a "squad." The squad was rigidly supervised by a "squad leader" who had been in the group for at least six months and had gone through intensive indoctrination. Discipline in the squads was strictly enforced, and recruits were not allowed even to go to the bathroom without permission from their leader. Drugs, tobacco, alcohol, and sex in any form were taboo in the group. Life in the commune was a daily grind of Bible classes and hard work which consisted, for the most part, of farming the commune's agricultural acreage.

But there were a few exceptionally bizarre touches, just so things wouldn't get too dull. Aside from Bible classes and chores, all members had to go through a "survival training course" administered by Brother Isaiah, which taught them how to survive in the wild, how to find water, what plants to eat, and so forth. This was necessary, according to Sievers, because the last days before the Judgment would be a time of great persecution for all Christians, and in order to survive, his followers were going to have to break up into small guerrilla bands and take to the hills to await the Second Coming, at which time Christ would appear and award them the earth to rule.

I finished and put the articles away before I threw up the dinner I had just eaten. It was a long way from the freewheeling, libertarian life-style of the Satan's Warriors to the fanatical, fascistic straitjacket existence of the members of the Word of God. Susan Gurney seemed to be swinging on a pendulum between emotional extremes. I was convinced more than ever that she had to be found before she completed the arc back the other way.

I paid my check and walked outside. It was just getting dark. The neon signs and theater marquees were winking on up and down the street. It was still early for the nightly parade of hookers and tricks and gays and pushers and freak-watchers who converged on Hollywood Boulevard to look for their respective connections, and foot traffic on the sidewalks was light. I left my car in the coffee shop parking lot and started walking east toward Vine.

As I approached Las Palmas, I spotted two of them across the street and stopped to watch. One was a Caucasian with short, brown hair and glasses; the other was a lanky black with a bushy Afro that sat on his head like a neatly clipped hedge. Both were dressed in long-sleeved, white shirts and ragged blue jeans. Each wore a shoulder-strapped pouch out of which protruded a black book that I took to be a Bible.

They had stationed themselves strategically on each side of the sidewalk so that anyone who walked the block had to encounter one of them. They stood stone-faced and grim, silently and mechanically thrusting their papers into passing hands. Occasionally, when someone refused to take a pamphlet, one of them would leave his post and follow the pedestrian up the street, shouting passages of scripture, until the stubborn sinner gave up and took the handout. But this rarely happened; most of the passersby already knew how the game was played and accepted the literature, only to drop it a block up. It was easier for them that way but hell on the city maintenance crew; the next block looked like New York in January.

I crossed the street at the light and walked toward them. The black eyed me as I approached. When I got within reach he stepped forward and pushed the paper into my hand. It was the same handout Haynes had given me at his house. I looked at it as if I had never seen it before. "What's this?"

"The Word, brother, the Word of the Lord Jesus Christ. The time of the return is here. Accept Him into your heart and be saved." His eyes were wide and his speech was rapid and excited, as if he were on speed.

"How long have you been saved?" I asked, to keep him going.

"One year, brother. One glorious year. I used to be a revolutionary. I used to think that the answer was in blowing things up. But then I got zapped by the Spirit and I found out that Jesus is the only true revolutionary." He waved a hand at the neon lights on the street. "All this will soon be blown to smithereens, anyway. The days of the Whore of Babylon are numbered. There isn't time for any of that other political jive, man, just for saving souls."

The other one, seeing that his partner had hooked a live one, left his position and joined us. He stared at me levelly for a few seconds before he spoke, his eyes looking grotesquely huge behind his thick glasses.

"Look around you, brother, if you don't believe the last days are upon us. The Bible says that in the last days, the sun will become black as sackcloth and the moon will turn red, like blood. It says the rivers will become bitter and poisoned and many will die from drinking their water. Look at the pollution today and you can see that it's all coming true. Our rivers are clogged with sewage, and soon the smog will be so thick that the sun will look black from down here."

I waved the pamphlet in his face. "I'm really interested in all this. Where can I find out more about it?"

"Come to our service tonight. We have a bus that leaves at seven from the corner of Cahuenga. It will bring you back after the service."

"Maybe I will; thanks."

I started to move off, but the kid with the glasses ran after me and grabbed my arm. "Stay with us until the bus comes, brother. We'll pray together for Jesus to enter your heart."

I took his wrist and loosened his grip from my arm. "Hands off the suit, brother," I said. "I don't have the bread to lay out for a cleaning bill."

"That's Satan's trick, tempting you with material things to take your attention off God," he said, grabbing my sleeve again.

"It must be Satan that's telling me to bust you in the mouth," I snarled. His eyes grew even larger behind the magnifying lenses, and he released his grip and stepped back. I saw my chance and started down the street.

"I'll pray for you, brother," he called after me. "Jesus loves you."

I walked back to the coffee shop parking lot and got my car. I kept to the back streets and came up Cahuenga and parked below Hollywood.

It was 6:45. A crowd of about 15 kids had already gathered at the corner. All but about five of them were wearing the same white linen shirts and Bible pouches. I watched with curiosity as five or six of the group clustered around a young boy who appeared to be a new convert. They were all talking to him at the same time, and he looked confused. Suddenly he got down on his knees and closed his eyes. The others gathered around him and put their hands on his head and shoulders and broke into some unintelligible chant that sounded like a recitation of vowels from the alphabet. After about two minutes of this they clapped their hands and shouted: "Thank you, Jesus." The boy got up. Everybody was smiling, and a nice-looking young girl came up and kissed him gently on the cheek, which must have been a reward for reciting his vowels correctly.

At seven on the nose a battered, red, white, and blue school bus with THE WORD OF GOD written on the sides in huge blue letters and plastered with "Have a Nice Forever" and "Smile: God Loves You" day-glo bumper stickers pulled to a stop at the corner. The converters piled on the bus with their convertees, and it turned around and headed up Cahuenga for the freeway.

The bus was an easy tail. I stayed a good quarter of a mile behind it all the way. At the interchange of the San Diego Freeway it swung off and drove north toward Bakersfield. As we headed out of the San Fernando valley and started up the Grapevine, singing began to drift back to me from the open windows of the bus. I would have sung with them, but I didn't know the words.

At Castaic Junction the bus turned and headed west on Highway 126. Soon the barren clay hills flattened out, and we dropped into a wide agricultural valley of orchards and tilled fields. The strong smell of citrus stung my nostrils. The highway was deserted except for the bus and myself, and I dropped back to a half-mile to keep from being noticed.

About six miles east of Fillmore the bus's right blinker began flashing and its taillights went out. I tromped on the accelerator, but by the time I got to the road, there was no sign of the bus. I turned right and started down the road.

I crossed a large trellis bridge and went past a series of tiny fruit stands that looked like they were made out of old produce boxes. I found myself in the middle of a tiny town in an advanced state of decay. Most of the buildings were dark and abandoned, hollow husks that stared onto the street with dead, empty eyes. The only signs of life came from a bar on the corner, where a couple of Mexican farm workers stood outside, talking and drinking beer. I pulled up next to them and stuck my head out the window, trying to make myself heard above the Mexican music that blared from a jukebox inside.

"The Word of God? La Palabra de Dios?"

One of them pointed down the cross street. I thanked him and turned down it. About half a mile beyond the town, I spotted the place. It would have been hard to miss. It was a complex of a half-dozen, barracks-like buildings, what had probably at one time been a migrant workers' camp. The buildings were surrounded by a high, cyclone fence which was covered by signs such as RE-PENT NOW! NO TIME LEFT! THE WICKED WILL BURN IN HELL! The bus was in the center of the courtyard in front of a building that was larger than the others. Parked beside it were two other school buses, a VW van, and a Ford station wagon, all painted red, white, and blue.

I drove down the road and pulled off into a dirt clearing and parked beneath a large oak tree. Then I locked up the car and started back on foot.

The service had begun by the time I reached the gates. The walls of the big building were shaking from hands clapping and feet stomping. What sounded like a dozen electric guitars, two dozen tambourines, and a hundred and fifty voices wailed together on a soul-shaking version of the Beatles' "Lucy in the Sky with Diamonds." I stood there for a minute, trying to figure out what it was about the song that sounded different. Then I had it: through some minor changes in the lyrics, "Lucy in the Sky with Diamonds" had become "Jesus in the Sky with Angels."

Nothing is sacred to these people, I thought as I went across the courtyard and opened the door to the first barracks—not even John and Paul and George and Ringo. Inside, the building was one long, undivided room with a hardwood floor. Rolled up against the walls were sleeping bags, and on top of each bag, neatly folded, was a pair of Levi's and a white linen shirt. There were no identifying marks on either the clothes or the sleeping bags, nothing betraying personal possession. At the far end of the

34

room was a bathroom which consisted of a toilet, a badly stained sink, and a curtainless shower stall the size of a small broom closet. The other dormitories were the same.

I went back to the main building where things had quieted down and sneaked around the side. I looked in through one of the open windows. The room was filled with two sections of metal folding chairs, maybe a hundred chairs in each section. The chairs faced a stage up front, which was cluttered with guitar amplifiers, a drum set, and an old, upright piano. A bony, hollow-eyed girl was on the stage, telling the congregation how she had been strung out on heroin and had turned to prostitution to feed her habit; but then she met Jesus and realized that He was a million times better high than junk.

"That's what Jesus is saying to you," she shouted. "If you're tired of being ripped off, accept me in your heart and I'll make you high."

Her audience responded with a few scattered "Hallelujahs" and "Praise the Lords," and she stepped down from the stage. She was followed by a young man who told a similar story about being lifted out of the mire by Jesus. Then a tall, pale man mounted the stage and took over the mike. He had wild, carrot-colored hair that was rapidly receding in front, and with a very minor makeup job he could have been a stand-in for Bozo the Clown.

"You have heard how Jesus Christ helped save these poor sinners," he said. "Why don't you let Him come into your life? Jesus wants you to come to Him. Come up and get saved. You, brother—" He pointed to a teenage boy sitting in the front row. "Come up and get saved. Now."

The boy hesitated but then responded to the command and stepped up to the stage.

"Kneel down, brother, kneel down to Jesus. Bless you, brother. Don't be bashful, brothers and sisters, come up and get saved. Jesus loves you."

One by one the seats in the front two rows emptied until there were about 20 people kneeling in front of the stage. The man with the carrot top looked down and lifted his arms, smiling. "Let us pray for these newly found souls," he said. He bowed his head, and those still seated in the folding chairs raised their right hands in the air, palms upward, and began a confused, garbled chanting that resembled the A-E-I-O-U recitation I'd heard on Hollywood Boulevard.

After a few minutes, he broke off the chanting and yelled "Amen!" into the microphone.

"Amen!" the congregation echoed.

He held up three fingers in the air and shouted: "Revolution!"

Everyone imitated the gesture. Then he curled the three fingers into a fist and screamed: "Spirit—"

"Power!" was the echoing cry.

The service was apparently over, and the people kneeling in front of the stage were now rising to their feet. The man announced that hot food would be served in a few minutes to anybody who was hungry, then he stepped off the stage. Everybody broke up into small groups and began to talk. I went around to the front door.

There was a cluster of eight or nine young people standing near the doorway, talking cheerfully, as I stepped through. One of them saw me walk in and nudged the man next to him. The group fell silent and stared. It must have been the suit that did it.

As I started toward them I spotted the orange-haired prayer leader coming toward me from the other side of the room. He was accompanied by the black militant who had tried to recruit me on Hollywood Boulevard, and the black was talking rapidly into his ear and pointing at me.

"You have come to get saved, brother," the orange-haired man said as he came up to me.

"Are you Sievers?"

"No," he said. "Brother Moses is not here tonight. He was feeling poorly and asked me to take over for him. I'm Brother Abraham, his first lieutenant." He paused and smiled knowingly. "Brother Joshua here told me about your encounter earlier in Hollywood."

"He did, huh?"

"Yes," he said. "And I know why you are here."

"I wouldn't call that a very miraculous example of divine omniscience. I'm looking for somebody."

"No," he said, "that's why you *think* you are here. The Lord works in mysterious ways. You cannot run away from Him. He has sent you to us to be saved."

I didn't know if he was just trying to sidetrack me, but the

36

pompous way in which he spoke irritated me. "Okay," I said. "I confess. I came to get saved. Only I want to be saved by the four-star general. I never had much faith in first looeys."

He gave me the smile of a martyr. "Why are you running from the Spirit, brother? You are running a dangerous course. I guarantee that if you don't accept Jesus here, right now, that you will be in jail, in the morgue, or in a mental institution within six weeks."

"Do I get to choose which?"

He wagged a finger at me warningly. "Your jokes are sending you straight to hell, brother."

"Soon, I hope. There's a guy who's already there who owes me fifty bucks I could sure use right now. Now look, 'brother,' let's cut out all this bullshit and go see Sievers."

"I told you," he said stiffly, "Brother Moses is ill."

He signaled to a burly kid standing nearby and whispered something in his ear. The kid and Brother Joshua, the black revolutionary, moved around me and planted themselves firmly at my back. I knew I had to do something fast if I didn't want to get the bum's rush.

"Now listen, pal," I said, "and listen good, because you're going to have to remember it all to tell Sievers. I'm a private detective who was hired by some angry parents to find their daughter. She's a runaway and she's underage and I have reason to believe that she's somewhere in this commune. I can go and place a call to the sheriff's department and they'd gladly come down here and take the place apart looking for her, if that's what you want. But I'm sure your Brother Moses, or whatever you call him, would be very upset with you when he found out that things could have been settled with a lot less trouble for everybody concerned."

He bit his lip. "Who is the girl?"

"I'll tell it to Sievers."

He bit his lip again and then said to the two behind me: "Keep an eye on him. I'll be right back."

He strode off. I stood silently with my two centurions. I tried smiling at them, but they just looked through me with wooden stares. Brother Abraham returned a few minutes later, looking anything but happy.

37

"Brother Moses will see you," he said. "You two, come with me."

We marched outside. When we got there, I said: "My car is just down the road. I'll follow you."

"My orders are to bring you. You'll come with us."

We went outside. He pointed to the station wagon.

"What? No white horses? I'm disappointed. The brochures said you were supposed to have white horses and shirts sprinkled with blood—"

"Just get in the car."

I shrugged and climbed in the back seat. Brother Joshua sat next to me, while the other one rode up front with Abraham. We drove through the gates and up the road, past the bar where the Mexicans were still out front.

The cloud cover had partially broken up. A full moon lighted our way past a series of broken-down shacks, their front yards littered with junk. Soon the shacks were replaced by orange groves as the road began a twisting ascent into the foothills. The trees stood thick and dark on both sides of the road. We went about a mile farther before a clearing opened in front of our headlights, and I saw the house standing at the base of some high, clay cliffs.

It was a white, four-story, Victorian mansion with a steeply sloped, high-peaked roof rising out of its center and a heavy round stone turret anchoring one wing. It had an elaborate lattice-work front, scalloped eaves, and leaded Tiffany windows that cut the moonlight into a thousand jewel-like sections. The house itself was a thing of beauty, but out here, in the middle of nowhere, surrounded by orange groves and barren gray mountains, it looked disturbingly surreal, as if it weren't part of the landscape but instead were hovering above it.

As we parked in the gravel driveway I noticed two ladders against the side of the house. Abraham signaled me out of the car, and I trudged up the wooden steps to the front door.

The door was opened by a short, bull-necked man dressed in the usual Word of God fare, except for the combat boots. His brown hair was crew-cut, and he had a tight-skinned, square-jawed face. He gave Abraham a questioning look, then said: "This the guy?"

"Right."

The short man pulled the door open, and we filed in past him into a dimly lit entrance hall. Ahead of us a heavy mahogany staircase rose out of the polished parquet floor and after a half a dozen steps turned back on itself and disappeared into the ceiling.

The short man with the boots closed the door and thrust out a hand, beckoning with short, meaty fingers. "Let's see some i.d."

I shrugged and pulled out my wallet and opened it to my photostat. I handed it over to him and said: "Just leave the credit cards, 'brother.' I haven't decided to join the fold yet."

His expression remained impassive while he looked over my license. "This way," he said, slapping it back into my hand.

He turned abruptly, and we followed him through a wide, carved mahogany portal into a large living room furnished with expensive-looking antiques. At the far end of the room a man stood in front of a large bay window, staring out at the dark valley below. He turned as we came in.

The man was tall. He had a full beard and long blond hair that gathered around his narrow shoulders. His complexion was clear and pale, and his features were cleanly handsome, almost chiseled, with prominent cheekbones and a thin, high-bridged nose. His blue eyes were pale and piercing in their coldness, edged by almost pure white lashes and brows. He wore a pair of old gray slacks, leather sandals over thick wool socks, and a hand-tooled Mexican shirt with fancy red embroidery on the collar.

He glanced at the short man who nodded his head slightly, then he turned to me. "I'm Aaron Sievers," he said. He spoke softly, but his voice was deep and resonant; there was unmistakable power in it.

"Jacob Asch," I said, holding out my hand.

He took it. His hand was cold and clammy. "I understand you're a detective."

"That's right."

He nodded, then turned to Abraham. "Wait outside."

"Won't you sit down?" Sievers asked amiably, motioning toward a brocaded chair. He sat on a velvet love seat opposite me while the short man who had answered the door remained standing behind him, eyeing me coolly.

"This is some house you have here," I said.

"Thank you. It was built in 1887 by a railroad millionaire from

Chicago who came to California for his health. He was the one who is responsible for having started most of the citrus agriculture in this area. G. I. Fedderson. We just purchased the house itself a year ago from what's left of his estate. We're in the process of restoring it, as you can see. When the upstairs is finished, it will serve as more living space for our members. The commune facilities down below are already overcrowded." There was a forced politeness in his voice, which was as fragile as a Dresden china teacup. "But you didn't come here to discuss this house. I understand you're looking for a missing girl."

"That's right."

"What makes you think she's here?"

"I don't know that she is. I *do* know that she was living here a few weeks ago."

He smiled and stroked his beard thoughtfully. "I see. Well, we always try to cooperate fully with the police and with the parents of our disciples. We always check strictly the ages of the youngsters that come to us. We realize what kind of trouble errors like that can cause us, especially since many people misunderstand our purposes here at the Word of God. Now, what did you say the name of this girl was?"

"I didn't," I said.

Sievers must have misconstrued my hesitation, because he immediately chimed in: "It's all right. Anything you have to say to me may be said in front of Brother Isaiah here. He is my chief lieutenant and my bodyguard."

"The girl's name is Susan Gurney. Around your commune, she was known as Sister Sarah."

He scowled. "Brother Abraham said you were looking for a juvenile runaway—"

"I told him that to make sure I got up here. Your Holiness is a very difficult man to see."

Isaiah dropped his arms to his sides and shifted his weight to the balls of his feet, but Sievers held up a hand and the tension that had stiffened the other man's body seemed to be held there, suspended. "You also told him that you were working for the girl's parents. Was that also a lie?"

I thought that one over quickly. I didn't think the mention of Haynes' name would strike the most responsive chord with Sievers. The last thing I wanted was for him to clam up on me now. "No, that wasn't a lie. I'm working for Eric Gurney, Susan's father."

Our eyes met for a few long seconds. His eyes were like blue ice. Somehow they seemed to reflect light without giving off any of their own. I began to feel uncomfortably naked under their steady gaze.

"You can go back and tell Mr. Gurney that his daughter is no longer here. She was forcibly abducted three weeks ago by the 10:36, Haynes, and an agent of Satan named Larry Farnsworth."

"10:36?"

"The Book of Matthew," he said in a condescending tone. "Chapter ten, verse thirty-six. 'Man's foes shall be they of his own household.'"

"Sorry, but I'm afraid my New Testament is a little weak. I had trouble enough getting through the Old one."

"Well, you had better sharpen it up," he said smiling. "You are surely going to need it for the End."

I tried not to react to his self-righteous spiel, although I found it took a solid effort. "I've talked to Haynes. He claims you brainwashed his stepdaughter."

"We only tried. We didn't succeed."

"Pardon me?"

He made an off-handed gesture. "Brainwashing is the whole point of what we are doing, Mr. Asch. Soul-pollution is the number one disease in the world today. Christ offered his blood so that the righteous may wash their brains and souls clean from the stain of corruption that has come to infect the world. We must not have succeeded with Sister Sarah. Otherwise, she would have come back to us."

"Then you haven't seen the girl since she was taken out of here?"

"No," he said. "If you really want to find her, I suggest that you try to locate Farnsworth. He is probably holding her prisoner somewhere, filling her full of Satan's lies."

"Was."

He cocked his head to one side, interested. "What do you mean, *was?*"

"Farnsworth deprogrammed Susan and turned her over to her mother and stepfather, but apparently she didn't stay deprogrammed. She ran away from home six days ago."

He looked up at Isaiah and said: "Did you hear that, brother? Clearly the work of the Lord. In His divine compassion He has intervened to snatch Sister Sarah from the clutches of the Demon."

"Praise the Lord," Isaiah interjected.

"Now we must wait and see if she returns to us. If she does, it will truly be a miracle of God."

"Praise the Lord," Isaiah repeated.

Their Paul Winchell-and-Jerry Mahoney-of-the-Latter-Day-Saints act was starting to get to me, but I went ahead. "Why do you say it will be a miracle if she comes back?"

"Because she wouldn't let Jesus into her life. When she was witnessed and first came here, she confessed to having committed the most obscene acts at Satan's bidding and said she wanted to be washed clean by the blood of Christ. But she held back, and the Spirit never entered her. If she had remained with us the Spirit might have taken her, but Satan saw what was happening and sent his emissary Farnsworth to intervene. Now she's wandering around out there, prey to the Devil and his snares."

"What kind of obscene acts did she confess to? You mean sexual?"

He gave me a knowing look. "That and other things. The girl was constantly obsessed by unclean thoughts. The Devil doesn't part easily with one of his children. But I never gave up on her, even after the trouble started—"

"What kind of trouble?"

He paused thoughtfully. "About a week before she was kidnaped, she was caught smoking a joint by one of the brothers. Drugs are strictly forbidden at the Word. He told her he was going to report her for it. She tried to seduce him to keep him from telling, but he reported the incident to Brother Abraham, anyway. I couldn't have the girl infecting the rest of the members with her wickedness, but at the same time I didn't want to expel her from the commune, knowing that it would be pushing her right into the arms of Satan. So I gave her the choice of leaving or doing penance for her sins. She decided to do penance and stay."

"What is penance?"

"Thirty days of closely supervised meditation, prayer, and fasting. I told her that at the end of that time, if she had not accepted Jesus into her life and repented her wickedness, she would have to leave."

"Did she repent?"

"Verbally, yes. But she hadn't yet given her life up to the Holy Spirit. That was the only thing that could have saved her. That's why I say it isn't likely that she will be back here. I'm afraid her soul is lost eternally to the fiery pit."

"Don't you think that judgment is a bit harsh, just for smoking a joint?"

"God is not love," he said, "contrary to what you might have been led to believe. That is Satan's line of propaganda to harvest souls. God wiped out the iniquitous in the Great Flood. He barbecued Sodom and Gomorrah. Does that sound like love to you? Everybody seems to think they can run around sinning and doing whatever they please and in the end, God will kiss them on the cheek and say, 'That's all right, I forgive you.' But they are falling right into the Devil's trap. It's all down in black and white for everyone to see; Romans 6:23—'For the wages of sin is death, but the gift of God is eternal life through Jesus Christ our Lord.'"

A bad actor would have raised his voice to match the fire-and-brimstone message, but the man's voice remained calm and low-keyed. If he was merely a con man who had found pushing Doom more profitable than selling cars, then he was a damn good con man, because that cold, fanatical light that shone in his eyes looked deadly serious.

"If drugs aren't allowed in your commune, where did she get the grass she was caught with? Do you know?"

He glanced over at Isaiah. "From a self-avowed member of Satan's storm troopers who visited her here several times. He belonged to an outlaw biker gang known as the Satan's Warriors."

"Do you remember his name?"

"I'm afraid I don't."

"Was it Gypsy?"

"It may have been. Now that I think about it, I believe it was."

"What did he look like?"

Sievers looked me over like a weight-guesser at a carnival. "He was about your height, maybe a little shorter. But lighter. He had long hair and a mustache. Unclean. Sister Sarah said he was an ex-convict."

"Did you ever see him again?"

"As a matter of fact, I did. He came back up here a couple of days after Sister Sarah was kidnaped, wanting to see her. I told him she wasn't here, but that even if she was, he wouldn't be allowed to see her because of what he had done. He didn't like that. He came back up the next day with some of his friends, threatening violence and demanding to see Sister Sarah."

"What happened?"

"Nothing," he said casually. "I convinced him that she was not here, and they went away."

I nodded and asked: "Was Susan friendly with anybody in particular while she was living here?"

"No," he said flatly. "She had problems adjusting to life here for that reason, as a matter of fact. She had trouble relating to the other members. Her attitude was basically defensive, not one that opened her up to many friendships."

"I'd like to talk to some of your members, if I could. Maybe one of them would know something that might help me find Susan."

He frowned and shook his head. "I'm afraid I couldn't allow that."

"Why not?"

"For the simple reason that I established the Word of God to enable those who might choose the path of righteousness to prepare for the Judgment and for the coming struggle with the Antichrist. To do that, they must be strong and pure, free from the contaminating influences of the outside world. You're a contaminating influence, Mr. Asch. You carry the Mark of the Beast there on your forehead."

He pointed a finger, and I involuntarily wiped a hand across my brow. "You can't wipe it off," he said. "It's there for eternity or until you fall down on your knees and pray to Jesus to be saved. I know. I used to traffic in the world of sin. I used to fall down before Satan the tempter when he held out fists full of money. But then God came to me in a blinding vision one day and threatened me with death unless I repented my wicked ways and started preaching the Word. He told me that only the righteous shall survive the Judgment and that all the rest, the cowardly and the unbelieving and the fornicators and the sorcerers and the idolators and all liars, shall be cast into the pit that burns with fire and brimstone."

44

That meant there was still a chance for me. I was only batting three out of six. "If I fall down on my knees and get saved, then can I talk to some of your members?"

His face darkened. "You talk like an atheist."

I shrugged. "'I find it very difficult to believe in a God less tolerant than I am.' The Gospel according to St. Somerset Maugham."

"You're not hurting me with your blasphemies, only yourself. God does exist and He is sitting judgment on your iniquities right now. The Bible says: 'Whoever speaks a word against the Son of Man, it shall be forgiven him, but whoever speaks against the Holy Spirit, it will not be forgiven him, either in this life or the other.'"

"I'll try to keep it in mind."

"You should," he said. "In the meantime, I'll pray for your soul." He rose out of his chair, a signal that our conversation was at an end. "I'm afraid I'm going to have to ask you to leave now. It's late, and I have a full schedule ahead of me tomorrow. Brother Abraham will drive you back to your car."

I stood up and started to offer my hand, but Isaiah took a quick step forward and clamped a vise-like grip on my elbow. Sievers said goodnight and turned his back on us, resuming his place in front of the window.

I wrenched my arm free of Isaiah's grip and said to Sievers' back: "One more question. If the world is going to go up in smoke the day after tomorrow, why are you bothering to have this house restored?"

He did not turn around. "The Lord ministers to me. My allotment is merely to obey."

Watching him stare out the window, I wondered what evil he saw lurking down there in the orange groves, what horrible demonic shapes he was molding out of the kaleidoscopic night. I didn't have much time to wonder. Isaiah's grip reattached itself to my elbow and I felt myself being guided firmly toward the door.

Isaiah steered me outside and waited on the front porch until I was wedged firmly between Joshua and his buddy before going back inside.

We drove back to the commune in silence. Abraham stopped the car in front of the gates. Joshua got out of the car and opened the door for me. After I was out, Abraham drove through the

45

gates and parked by the main building. Joshua closed and pad-locked the gates, then walked over to where Abraham and the other brother were getting out of the car.

As I walked back to my own, I noticed that the Salvation bus was still parked in the courtyard. Whoever had come out here on it expecting to get back to Hollywood tonight had better start offering incense to Lucifer.

CHAPTER SIX

The smoker's hack on the other side of the wall woke me up at 7:30 as usual. I rolled over and waited for it to stop, but this morning it didn't, so I finally said to hell with it and got up. I went into the bathroom and splashed some cold water in my face. By the time I came back out and put on the coffee, the coughing had subsided.

For the two months I had lived in the building, I had been awakened almost every morning by the same anonymous, phlegm-choked death rattle without ever seeing to whom it belonged. One day soon I was going to have to get a face to go along with that cough. I was going to have to go next door and say, Hello there, Mr. (or Mrs.) Cough, I'm your next-door neighbor. Please accept this package of Smith Brothers with my kindest regards and allow me to help you move your goddamn bed away from the wall. Someday, but not today. Today I had other things to do. I poured myself a cup of coffee and sat down at the phone.

Eric Gurney answered his phone at home. He balked at first when I explained to him who I was and what I was doing but finally gave in and told me to come to his office at the United Mutual Insurance Company at 9:30. I then tried Larry Farnsworth again. His line was still busy. I dialed the operator and told her I was Dr. Blacker and that I had a patient with a coronary problem at that number, and I needed an emergency verify. She checked it out and told me that the line was out of order. I didn't like that. I called Farnsworth's answering service back and asked the girl there how long had it been since Mr. Farnsworth had checked in. She said four days. When I asked if that was usual, she admitted grudgingly that it wasn't, that he usually checked in once or twice a day.

I sat for a few minutes, staring into the dregs at the bottom of my coffee cup, trying to analyze the uneasy feeling in the pit of my stomach. Then I got out my address book and looked up the number for Jerry Newcomb.

Jerry was a computer programmer at TRW who made a little extra pocket money by cashing in on friendships he had nurtured with select people at the telephone and utilities companies. His wife answered the phone.

"Hello?"

"Is Jerry there?"

"Just a minute," she said, then Jerry picked it up.

"Glad I caught you at home, Jerry. This is Jake Asch."

"Oh, hi, Jake. I was just getting ready to leave for work. What can I do for you?"

"Got a piece of paper and a pencil handy? I'm going to give you a number."

"Got one right here. Shoot."

"627-5912. It's unlisted. It belongs to a guy by the name of Larry Farnsworth. I need an address."

"How soon?"

"As soon as you can get it."

"Hmm. It's 8:15 now. My contact won't be in the office until after nine."

"I'll call you back around ten or so."

"That should be okay. Call me at work. You've got the number."

"Have your rates gone up or is it still twenty-five?"

"Still twenty-five."

"Will a check be all right?"

"Sure," he said. "You're always good, Jake; you know that."

I said good-bye and hung up, then put my mug in the sink and folded the bed back into its couch form without making it. I took a leisurely shower and shaved, then got dressed and went out to the car.

The weather had cleared during the night. Only a few isolated clouds hung in the crisp, smogless sky. Maybe it was an omen for my case, but I doubted it. The queasy, churning feeling was still there in the pit of my stomach.

The United Mutual Insurance Company occupied the eleventh and twelfth floors of a 14-story, glass-sheeted building that rose out of Wilshire's Miracle Mile. I parked in the underground lot and took the elevator up to the twelfth floor.

Eric Gurney's official title turned out to be Operations Vice-President, which meant that he oversaw the overseers at Mutual's L.A. branch. The office was spacious but not oversized, handsomely decorated in bright colors. Gurney was standing behind a large walnut desk as I came in. Behind him the windows offered a panoramic view of the city, at least until the smog returned.

We shook hands. Gurney's palm was cool and moist, but his handshake was firm. "Sit down," he said curtly.

I took a chair in front of the desk and studied the man. He was a well-groomed man in his middle forties, with a strong, deeply cleft chin and unsmiling gray eyes. His brown hair was brushed back from his wide forehead and conventionally parted on one side. He was smartly dressed in a navy blue gabardine suit that looked as if it had never been creased, a pink shirt, and a dark blue tie.

After he had settled back down in his swivel chair, he said: "I'm afraid I don't understand exactly why you wanted to see me, Mr. Asch. As I told you on the phone, I haven't seen Susan in months."

"When exactly was the last time you saw her, Mr. Gurney?"

"In June, just before she was supposed to graduate."

"That was right before she ran away?"

He lifted an eyebrow and stared at me coldly. "Are you asking me or telling me?"

"Asking you."

"I wouldn't know when she ran away."

I smiled. It probably looked forced. "Where did you see her?"

"Here at the office," he said, lifting his hand off the desk.

"Did you know then that she was planning to go to live at the Word of God commune?"

"No. The first I heard of it was when Bob Haynes called me a few days ago."

"I hear you and your ex-wife had a disagreement over them hiring someone to pull Susan out of the commune—"

"That's right," he said. "I don't believe in dictating to anyone what their religious convictions should be. Susan is old enough to make those kinds of decisions for herself."

49

"Robert Haynes claims she wasn't. He says she was brain-washed."

"That's a bunch of crap."

"You don't believe it?"

"No, I don't."

"And you wouldn't have any qualms about your daughter living at a commune like the Word of God."

"Not if she was sure that's what she wanted—no. Personally, I think it was just a phase she was going through. She would have come out of it after a little while and gotten onto a less extreme track." He stopped and then added: "I could think of a lot worse places for her to be."

"Do you know much about the group?"

"A little. I've done some checking. They're doing a lot of good work rehabilitating drug addicts and things like that. I'd rather see her out there than in the hands of someone like Larry Farnsworth, believe me."

"Why do you say that?"

He looked at me sternly. "Because I know the man, and I know what he's like."

"How do you know him?"

"He did some ten percenting for the company a few years back, a couple of salvage jobs, recovering some stolen merchandise. That was before he started all this deprogramming business."

"I thought he was a private detective."

"He was until he got his license pulled."

"How did that happen?"

"He was hired by some big company to do some spying on a rival corporation and thought he could make a killing by playing both sides of the fence and selling information to both companies. He got caught at it. The state board pulled his license for breaking the fiduciary interest."

"How did he get into the deprogramming business?"

"I have no idea," he said. "All I know is that he's a shady son of a bitch. He doesn't care what he has to do or who he has to hurt, as long as there's a dollar in it."

I nodded. "Getting back to Susan, Mr. Gurney, I was hoping that you might be able to give me some background information on her."

"What kind of information?"

"Anything at all about her past, what she's like."

"Why?"

"Because as things stand, all I've got to go on is an 8 x 10 graduation picture. I don't know what's motivating her, and without that, I have very little chance of finding her."

He swiveled his chair slightly to one side so that he was watching me obliquely. "Why come to me? Cynthia hired you. I'm sure she gave you a detailed picture of Susan's personal history, as warped as that picture may be."

"That's why I was hoping you could straighten me out," I said as amiably as possible. The man's abrasiveness was beginning to rub me raw. "Your ex-wife isn't very communicative about Susan's past, especially when that past involves you. As a matter of fact, she threatened to fire me if I talked to you."

A new curiosity dawned in his eyes, but the hostility had not disappeared from his voice. "Then why are you?"

"Because I thought you might be interested in helping Susan. For her sake, it may be important that she's found and found soon."

He came forward in his seat. The light slanting through the windows behind him threw dark lines of worry across his face. "What do you mean by that?"

"Your daughter has been running around with an odd assortment of weirdos, Mr. Gurney—Jesus freaks, convicted felons, bike bums. I have information that she may be running with one of the Satan's Warriors she was arrested with last year, and in her current state of mind, that might spell trouble. She got probation the last time. Next time, she may not be so lucky."

"So what am I supposed to do about it?"

"Nothing," I said. "Just sit here and wait for her to get picked up for vagrancy or possession or something more serious so that you and your ex-wife can point fingers at one another and gloat and say, 'I told you so.' What more could Susan expect from her parents?"

It was probably a little strong. But between Gurney and his ex-wife, I was working myself into a pretty strong mood. Besides, I was hoping the shock value of it might loosen him up.

He stiffened as if I had hit him across the mouth with a wet washcloth. I thought for a second he was going to start yelling for me to get out of his office, but he didn't. He just took a deep breath and exhaled slowly, then rubbed the lower half of his face nervously with his hand. "What do you want to know?"

"From what I gather, Susan has psychological problems. If I knew what the source of those problems was, I could get a better picture of what's driving her."

"The source?" he asked incredulously. "You're working for it."

"You mean her mother, I take it."

He nodded.

"What was the problem?"

"There wasn't just one problem. There was a myriad of them. Cynthia is a sick woman. She's always resented Susan, regarded her as a burden, even before she was born."

"I'm afraid I don't understand," I said.

"Cynthia never wanted a child. The thought of it terrified her. She used to have recurring nightmares about dying during child-birth, and it made her frigid. She only got pregnant after our marriage had already begun to disintegrate, as a last-ditch effort to try to hold onto me."

"Obviously things didn't work out."

He made a frustrated gesture with one hand and said: "I tried to stick it out for Susan's sake, but life with Cynthia wasn't a marriage; it was a daily battle with her anxieties. And then, by that time, I'd met Elaine—"

"Elaine?"

"My present wife," he said and paused. "I saw a chance to be happy and took it. Cynthia has never forgiven me for that."

"How old was Susan then?"

"Four."

"And your wife was awarded custody?"

"It was part of the settlement," he said with a pained expression. "I should have fought her, but Cynthia threatened to contest the divorce if I tried. I was just an agent with the company then, and she knew I couldn't afford a long-drawn-out court battle."

"And she could?"

"My ex-wife is a wealthy woman. She inherited a small fortune from her grandfather's estate when she was in her early twenties. She would have used every penny of it to make sure I didn't get Susan."

"Why? If she resented Susan like you say, why didn't she just let you have her?"

"Because she's sick. She wanted to use Susan as a tool to get revenge on me for leaving her."

Under normal circumstances I would have thought the man was suffering from some sort of persecution complex, but after talking with his ex-wife, I wasn't so sure. "Did you see Susan much after the divorce?"

His eyes skirted mine and lighted in a corner of the room. "I wouldn't say often—no—I was supposed to have visitation rights on weekends, but Cynthia made sure it was very few weekends. Those times I was supposed to come over and pick her up, Cynthia would go to Palm Springs or somewhere for the weekend and take Susie with her."

"You could have gotten a court injunction to stop her."

He shrugged hopelessly. "The situation was difficult. Elaine and I had children of our own by that time, and Susie didn't get along with Karen, our oldest. It just seemed better to leave things as they were."

He scowled suddenly as if catching the hollow sound of his own rationalization. Before he could revert to his former defensive hostility, I said: "On the times you saw her, did Susan talk about her home life to you?"

He hesitated, then said: "All the time. As a matter of fact, that's about all she ever did talk about. She would tell me that her mother didn't love her and that she wanted to move in with Elaine and me. That was impossible, of course."

"Haynes told me that she used to run away and go over to your house."

"That's right," he said, nodding. "We'd let her spend the night and then pack her back off to her mother's in the morning. I always felt as if I were betraying her somehow, sending her back to Cynthia. She'd always put up such a protest about it, crying and whining. There wasn't anything else we could do; it's hard to explain the law to kids that age. They just don't understand what it means."

"How old was she when she stopped coming over?"

"I don't know. About ten or eleven, I guess. It was around the time Cynthia married Haynes."

I nodded. "How come Haynes has stuck it out so long with your ex-wife?"

He raised an eyebrow. "Bob Haynes used to be a stockbroker. And he wasn't doing too well at it, from what I understand."

"What does he do now?"

"Nothing that I know of," he said, then added quickly: "I don't mean it to sound like I'm knocking the guy. I like Bob Haynes, in fact. I don't blame him for succumbing. Even I nearly did. Cynthia is very adept at the carrot and the stick. She pestered me constantly while we were married to quit the company and live off her money. But I knew that once I got into that, she'd have me right where she wanted me, and I'd never get out."

He was hitting close to home. I felt a tiny twinge of shame when I thought about what I was doing here. "How did your daughter get along with Haynes?"

"On the times I saw them together, fine. He seemed to treat Susan with a genuine affection."

"On the times you saw Susan lately, what did you talk about?"

"Oh, I don't know. Things." He paused, then looked down at his hand on the desk top. "Actually, we'd grown apart in the past few years. We didn't see each other much and when we did, things were kind of strained between us."

"When she came to your office in June, what were the circumstances of her visit?"

He hesitated. "She wanted to borrow a hundred dollars."

"Did she say what for?"

"She said she wanted to buy some art supplies. She said she was taking up painting, but her mother wouldn't give her the money."

"Did you give it to her?"

"Yes, I did," he said, frowning. "I was going to give her a present for graduation anyway, so I figured she might as well have it then."

"Did you believe her story about why she wanted the money?"

"I did at the time. I realize now she probably wanted to use it to run away on."

Watching him, I had the feeling that if his daughter had come to him asking for a thousand dollars to buy an electric train, he would have given it to her. Money was the easiest and quickest way he knew to try to buy off the guilt he felt for having abandoned her as a child. But a hundred or a thousand—it wouldn't have made any difference. The guilt would have still been there, as it was now, demanding payment.

I put my pen away. "Well, thanks for talking to me, Mr. Gurney. I appreciate it. I'd also appreciate it if you'd keep this conversation to yourself. I wouldn't want it to get back to your ex-wife that I talked to you. It won't help Susan if I get fired."

He nodded but didn't say anything. I took out a card and handed it to him. "In case you hear anything from Susan and you want to get in touch with me, you can reach me at this number."

He stared blankly at the card for a few seconds, then put it down on the top of the desk. "What are you going to do when you find her?"

"Nothing. My job is just to find her and report to Robert Haynes."

He bit his lip and said: "If you find her and she does need some help of some kind, I'd like to know about it. I realize it's rather late, but I'd like to do something for Susan if I could."

"I understand, Mr. Gurney," I said, standing. "I'll let you know what happens."

He seemed relieved by this and stood up, offering me his hand. I took it and said good-bye and took the elevator downstairs to the lobby. I located a pay phone and called Jerry Newcomb. He gave me an address for Farnsworth at 522 Verdugo Road, Apartment 3A, Los Angeles. I told him I would drop him a check in the mail and took the elevator down to the garage.

CHAPTER SEVEN

The apartment building sat on the top of a dome-like hill over-looking the man-made lake of Echo Park. It was a yellow, U-shaped stucco job. Although it was by no means new, it looked startlingly modern in contrast to the other small, neo-Victorian houses on the block, which would have been in fashion when Amy Semple MacPherson was preaching holy hellfire in her Angelus Temple down the street.

I parked my car across the street and got out. The building had an open courtyard crisscrossed by cement paths that cut their way through dichondra grass and ferns and ran to tunneled stair-ways in the side of the building. I went up the walk to the third tunnel and trudged up the stairs.

At the top of the stairs, Apartment 3A faced Apartment 3B from across a small landing. I pressed the buzzer on the door. No answer. I pressed it again, waited, then knocked. I went back down the stairs to the courtyard.

After some wandering around, I found the passageway that led to the parking area out back and went through it. In the parking space allotted to Apartment 3A was a 1967, red, Pontiac convert-ible. I tried the door, but it was locked.

I went back through the courtyard and up the stairs once more. This time, I tried the buzzer for 3B. There was no answer there, either. I stepped back across the landing and inspected the door. There were no dead locks on the door that I could see, so I took out my wallet and extracted my plastic lock-picking card and pushed on the door while I wriggled it into the crack. I worked the card against the jamb until I had the tongue of the lock pressed back. Then I pushed the door open.

A rush of stifling, hot air blew against my face, carrying with it the unmistakable, indescribable stench of decaying flesh. I gagged but managed to keep from vomiting and reached quickly around the door and unlocked it from the inside, then pulled it closed. I went back down a couple of steps trying to escape the smell, but some of it followed me. I stood there, trying not to breathe through my nose, fighting the urge to get the hell out of there. I took a handkerchief out of my coat pocket and went back up to the landing and opened the door.

The living room was small and dismal. A brown couch and two matching chairs were grouped near a low, rectangular coffee table in the middle of the room, and the couch was anchored down on both ends by a pair of old lamps whose white shades were turning brown and brittle from years of hundred-watt heat. A portable television sat against one wall underneath some bookshelves lined with worn paperbacks. A formica-topped counter separated the living room from the kitchen, and to the left of that was a tiny breakfast nook area filled by a plastic breakfast table and chairs. That was where he was lying, his upper torso in the kitchen, his feet underneath the breakfast table.

He wasn't a pretty sight. The heat in the room had speeded decomposition right along, and the skin on his face and hands that was exposed to the air was blackish-green and swollen and suppurating pus. The wooden handle of a carving knife protruded from his bloated belly. All of the internal muscles had relaxed in death and there was a large, dark stain around the legs where the shit and urine had drained out of the body and soaked into the carpet.

Beside him was the reason his line had been busy. The telephone was lying on its side off the hook, where it had fallen from the stand at the end of the counter. I looked past him into the kitchen.

Bloody handprints smeared the sideboards by the sink and ran in streaks down the side of the wooden cupboards. A blood-soaked dishrag lay in the corner where it had been casually tossed. It looked as if it was what had been used to write the message on the door of the refrigerator. JESUS SAVES.

I was half-tempted to go through the pockets of the dead man to see if I could find some identification, but I squashed the thought. At that stage of putrefaction, a corpse is a deadly carrier of gas-producing bacilli, and I could think of other things I needed right now more than a good case of gangrene poisoning. I went back into the living room.

I was already perspiring freely from the oppressive heat in the room and went to the thermostat on the wall to check it out. Someone had turned the heat up to ninety, maybe someone with a personal grudge against the coroner.

There were two bedrooms at the end of the hall. One had been converted into an office. I started with it. From the looks of things, Farnsworth had needed a secretary. Papers were strewn across the desk top and overflowed onto the floor.

I poked through the top papers with my finger. There were some unpaid bills, a couple of letters from attorneys demanding payment for past-due legal fees, and some letters from distraught parents, asking Farnsworth to help them get their children back from assorted religious communes. The drawers contained the standard fare in stationery, but in one of them I did find something of mild interest: Farnsworth's checkbook.

Either the deprogramming business wasn't all it was cracked up to be or Larry Farnsworth was keeping all of his money in Swiss banks. He had a balance of $487.50 in his account, which was not an extravagant amount by any stretch of the imagination. But it was the third entry from the last that grabbed my attention. On September 18, six days earlier, Farnsworth had deposited $500 in the bank and under the space marked "Description of Item," he had written, "Investigation—R. Haynes." I looked back through the other entries and found that on September 4, Farnsworth had deposited $1,000, this one marked, "Deprogram.—S. Haynes."

I put the checkbook back in the desk and went into the bedroom. Things were in the same state of disarray in there. Farnsworth had been about as good a housekeeper as he was a filing clerk. Half the bureau drawers were pulled open and the sleeves of shirts hung carelessly over their sides. The bed was unmade. On it lay several wire coat hangers and a pair of wrinkled slacks. On the table by the bed was a paperback copy of a *Man from O.R.G.Y.*, spread face down like the wings of a dead bird.

After going through the drawers and the closet in the bedroom and coming up with nothing, I went into the bathroom and found more of the same: toothbrush, shaving cream and after-shave, a safety razor, and a hairbrush clogged with strands of dark brown hair.

I went back to the living room and took a peek out the front door to make sure the coast was clear. I stepped out onto the landing, making sure the door was locked from the inside before shutting it, and went down the stairs.

The mailboxes said that the manager's name was R. Tilden and that he lived in Apartment 6A. I went up the stairs and pressed the buzzer. The door opened immediately as if he had been waiting behind it, anticipating the ring.

He was a tall, gangly man with red-brown hair and a conspicuous gap between his two front teeth. His face was well weathered and dotted with freckles, as were his hands, which were large and big-knuckled and raw-looking. He wore a pair of paint-stained slacks and a long-sleeved plaid shirt which was also dotted with paint.

"You the manager?" I asked. My voice sounded as if I had sinus trouble; I realized I was still breathing through my mouth. The smell still lingered in my mind, and I found that it took a conscious effort to let go and breathe normally.

"That's right," he said, giving me some of the gap. "What can I do for you?"

"I've been trying to reach Mr. Farnsworth in Apartment 3A for the last two days, but his phone is out of order. I just went up and knocked on his door, but he doesn't answer."

He gave me a puzzled look. "So? He probably went away for a few days and doesn't know about his phone. I'll report it—"

"His car is out back."

He gave me another puzzled look and said: "So?"

"So I think something is wrong."

"Look," he said, making a defeated gesture with his hands, "he probably left with somebody else and left his own car here."

"That's logical," I said.

"Sure it is," he said, looking pleased with himself.

"But it doesn't explain the smell."

"What smell?"

"The smell coming from the other side of the door. Like there's somebody—or something—dead in there."

It took a couple of seconds for the impact of what I had said to sink in. When it did, his eyes widened excitedly, and he made a waving motion in the air with his hand. "Just a minute. I'll get my keys."

He disappeared from the door and when he reappeared, he was holding a ring full of keys. The smell was faint, but still present on the landing when we got to Farnsworth's apartment.

"You smell it?"

He sniffed the air and made a face. "Yeah. Maybe a cat or something got into the apartment and died. It happens sometimes."

"If it's a cat, it must be a big one."

"Yeah," he agreed. "It's a wonder Mrs. Cavendish hasn't said anything about it. She lives here in 3B. She raises hell about everything else."

He put the key in the door and turned the handle. I knew what was coming and held back a couple of stairs. The door opened a crack and he got a whiff of it and let go of the handle and grabbed his face.

"Shit," he blurted out, careening back against Mrs. Cavendish's door. "Something's dead in there, all right."

He stood there for a minute, his eyes excited and frightened. It looked as if he were having second thoughts about his big-cat theory.

"We'd better go in and see," I said as a word of moral encouragement.

"Yeah," he said, and after hesitating, went through the door. I followed him into the living room.

He stood in the center of the room for a few seconds, frozen, as if scared to go on. I tapped him on the shoulder and pointed into the breakfast nook. "Over there," I said and walked around to the kitchen counter, just to make it look good. "He's dead, all right."

I turned back around, but Tilden hadn't moved. He was still standing in the middle of the living room.

"We'd better get the cops over here," I said, but he didn't answer. When I looked at his face, I knew why. It was beet-red and his eyes were starting to protrude from their sockets.

"Breathe through your mouth," I told him, but it was too late.

He let go of the air he was holding in a noisy rush and then reflexively, he sucked in a lungful of the fetid apartment air to take its place. He emitted a half-scream, half-groan and bolted toward the door with a hand over his mouth.

He had just reached the door when everything came up. He rebounded from wall to wall down the stairway. I followed, stepping daintily through the messy trail he had left, thinking that Mrs. Cavendish was going to have something else to bitch about when she got home.

When I got to the bottom of the stairs, he was dry-heaving in the ferns. "I'll call the police," I said. "Your apartment open?"

He turned a greenish face up to me and nodded, then doubled over again in convulsions. I went up to his apartment and dialed the police.

CHAPTER EIGHT

While the coroner's men were upstairs in 3A trying to work what was left of Farnsworth into a plastic bag for transport downtown, I was in the manager's apartment, going over my story with a detective sergeant from L.A. homicide by the name of Williams. He was a middle-aged, pot-bellied man with mustard stains on the lapels of his Robert Hall suit. Having obviously read his police manual carefully about the importance of not antagonizing witnesses, he was effusively polite and smiled incessantly as he listened to my abridged version of how I happened to find Farnsworth's body. But we both knew that the smiles were *just* police manual, the politeness was just superficial, and that they would both be dropped like a wet sack of cement the minute he found an inconsistency in my story.

He waited patiently for me to finish my narration, then stared at what he had written in his notebook and nodded slowly. "I'm afraid I'm not quite clear on what your relationship was with the victim," he said after awhile. "Were you a friend of his?"

"No, I'd never met him."

"But you say you had been trying to reach him by phone since yesterday—"

"That's right."

"What about?"

"He was involved in a case I'm working on, and I wanted to talk to him about it."

He looked up from his notebook. His right eye was watching my face while his left was looking somewhere over my right shoulder. I wasn't sure that he was not doing that on purpose. The effect was positively disconcerting. "What kind of case?"

"A runaway-daughter job. Farnsworth ran a racket he called 'deprogramming.' What it was essentially was kidnaping young

62

kids from religious communes and holding them incommunicado while he worked on their heads, trying to get them to renounce their new-found religion and come back to so-called normalcy. The parents of the kids were the ones who would hire him to do it—at a thousand bucks a throw."

"That could be the tie-in with the writing on the wall," he mused more to himself than to me. "So what's it got to do with your case?"

"Farnsworth was hired a few weeks ago by my clients to snatch their daughter out of a Jesus freak commune where she'd gone to live and to run her through his little course. She came through it okay, but then a few days after she came home, she ran away again. The parents hired me to try to track her down."

He scribbled something in his notebook, then looked up. "So what were you coming over here to see Farnsworth about?"

"I was hoping he could tell me something that might help me find her."

"Like what?"

"I don't know."

He shifted in his chair and asked: "You see any connection between Farnsworth being murdered and the girl's disappearance?"

"No."

"I wouldn't expect you to say anything else," he said flatly. "I'm going to want the parents' names."

I thought about my options and saw that I had none that meant anything. "Mr. and Mrs. Robert Haynes. They live at 1055 Macedonia Way. That's in Olympian Estates."

"And the daughter's name?"

"Susan Gurney."

He took it down. "How come a different name?"

"Her parents are divorced, and her mother remarried Haynes. The real father is a guy by the name of Eric Gurney. He's an operations vice-president at United Mutual Insurance over in Wilshire."

"You say Farnsworth snatched the girl from some commune," Williams said. "What commune?"

"It's a Jesus freak commune over near Fillmore, called the Word of God. The head honcho is a guy named Aaron Sievers."

"You been out there?"

"Yes."

63

"You talk to this Sievers?"

"I talked to him."

"He mention Farnsworth?"

"Only in passing."

"What did he say?"

"Just that Farnsworth was an agent of the Devil and that he hadn't seen the Gurney girl since she'd been kidnaped from the commune."

"What do you think about that writing on the wall?"

"I don't know."

"You think this Sievers might have gotten bugged by Farnsworth snatching his converts and sent somebody to waste him?"

"It's possible, I guess. They're a pretty militant bunch of freaks out there. But I don't really see a strong motive. Sievers is knocking down fifteen grand a month with that commune of his. I can't see him risking that just to get rid of Farnsworth. In the long run Farnsworth probably netted him more converts than he was taking away just from the publicity he was generating."

"Maybe," he said. "But Sievers didn't have to have ordered the hit necessarily. Maybe one of his members thought he would be doing God and his guru a big favor by getting rid of the guy. Those people hear voices all the time, from angels and Jesus and all sorts of things, telling them to do all sorts of weird shit."

"It could have happened that way," I admitted. "But the Word of God wasn't the only Jesus freak group Farnsworth was taking his clients from. Or it could have even been some nut who read about the guy in the papers and saw himself as the Angel of Death coming to avenge the Lord. That sort of thing happens all the time."

He nodded and draped his arm over the back of the chair he was sitting in. "What do you know about Farnsworth?"

I repeated what Eric Gurney had told me, and he listened with interest. When I had finished he said: "Is that all you know about him?"

"You want his social security number?"

He smiled. "You wouldn't have any ideas about holding anything back from me, would you?"

"What could I possibly be holding back, sergeant? I just started on the case yesterday."

He watched me silently for a few seconds and said: "Okay, you can go. But stay available. I'm going to need a statement."

"Sure," I said, standing up and holding out my hand. For some reason he seemed surprised by the gesture. It took him a little while to regroup his thoughts and shake hands. I left him there and went down the stairs.

CHAPTER NINE

I drove down to Alvarado to the Hollywood Freeway and got on it, heading north. I took the Sunset exit and stopped at the first pay phone and dialed Haynes' number. He answered the phone. I told him that something had come up and that I wanted to see him. He said to come right up. Twenty minutes later, I was ringing his doorbell.

Apparently the Mexican housekeeper had not been fired yet, because she opened the door. She led me through the living room and out to the pool, where Haynes was lying on a chaise lounge in his swimming trunks, soaking up the sun.

He stood as I came through the sliding glass door and came over to me, holding out his hand. His face looked more rested than when I had last seen him, and his eyes were clear and undimmed by alcohol.

"I was just going for a swim when you called," he said. "Why don't we sit out here and talk?"

He led me over to a pair of wrought iron patio chairs and I sat down on one of them. He took a towel from the back of the chaise lounge where he had been lying and draped it over his shoulders, then came over and took the other chair.

"What is it you wanted to see me about? You've found out something about Susan?"

"No," I said and then paused. "I was just over at Farnsworth's apartment. I went over there to talk to him about Susan, but he wasn't in a talkative mood. He was dead."

The impact of what I had said penetrated through to him and he looked at me in disbelief. "Dead?"

"Murdered."

"My God, that's awful. Who would want to murder Larry Farnsworth?"

"I don't know. Maybe one of the Jesus freak groups he was waging war against. Whoever killed him wrote 'Jesus Saves' in Farnsworth's blood on the wall."

He looked as if he were going to be sick.

"The police will probably be here to ask you about it tomorrow. I just wanted you to hear it from me before they show up."

The nausea passed from his face, replaced by startled concern. "You don't mean you told them about Susan?"

"I didn't have any choice."

"What do you mean, you didn't have any choice?"

"I found the body. That meant I had to report it. The police naturally wanted to know what I was doing knocking on Farnsworth's door in the first place. I had to tell them."

He made an irritated gesture with his hand and said: "You're supposed to protect your clients, not open them up to police harassment—"

"You've been reading too many detective novels, Mr. Haynes. To a homicide cop, murder cuts across a lot of employer-client relationships. If I want to keep working in this town, I have to have at least the passive approval of the police. If I started holding back information from them on a murder case and they found out about it—which eventually they would—they'd get on my back and never get off."

"I don't see why you had to report the thing in the first place. Why didn't you just get out of there and let somebody else report it?"

"Because if somebody happened to spot me going up to Farnsworth's apartment and just happened to report it to the cops, I'd have a lot more to answer for than I do now."

He groaned miserably and slumped back in his chair. "Do you realize what Cynthia is going to say when she sees the police up here?"

He stared out over the still, turquoise water, his face drowning in self-pity and for that moment, I pitied him, too. He was a weak little man trapped by his own aspirations and self-doubts.

"If you would like to terminate my services," I said, "we could figure things up now. Two days and expenses should come to somewhere around $300. I'll write you out a check for the other $200 if you'd rather look for someone else—"

He seemed startled by the suggestion. "No, no, of course not. I understand your position in this thing. It's a ticklish situation, obviously. It just took me by surprise, you telling me about the police and all. No, of course I want you to stay on the job."

"What about your wife?"

"What about her?"

"She may not feel the same way."

"Don't worry," he said. "I'll take care of Cynthia."

"Where is she, by the way?"

"She still isn't feeling well," he said absently. "She's in bed." He grew thoughtful for a minute, then said: "What exactly did you tell the police?"

"Nothing much. They wanted to know what I knew about Farnsworth. Since I didn't know much, I couldn't tell them much. I didn't tell them that Farnsworth was looking for Susan at the time he was killed."

I waited to see how he would take that. He nodded and pursed his lips pensively but didn't say anything.

"Was he?"

"Was he what?"

"Was he looking for Susan?"

He rubbed a brown, hairy hand nervously across his mouth. "I don't know what you mean."

"You told me Farnsworth had checked out the Word of God after Susan ran away the second time, to make sure that she hadn't gone back there. Did you authorize him to search farther than that?"

"Why should I?" he asked, hedging. "That's what I hired you for."

"I just thought that since Farnsworth used to be a detective, maybe you figured that two of us would have a better chance of tracking her down than just one."

"No," he answered, but his voice sounded uncertain.

"You're not being honest with me."

"But I am—"

"You paid Farnsworth a flat fee of one thousand dollars to abduct and deprogram Susan, right?"

"Yes, that's right," he said, licking his lips.

"And that was when?"

"I don't know. Three weeks ago or so. I can't remember exactly."

"Then what did you pay him five hundred dollars for on September 18?"

His face registered alarm. He leaned forward in his chair. "How did you know I paid Farnsworth $500?"

"While I was in Farnsworth's apartment, before the police arrived, I got a look at his checkbook. On September 18 Farnsworth made a deposit in his checking account for $500, and under the entry for the description of the deposit, he had your name."

"Who's got the book now?"

"The police," I said, "and they'll want to know about it, too." I gave him a chance to answer. When he didn't, I gave him another nudge. "Look, Haynes, if Susan is involved in any way in this thing, there's no way you're going to be able to shield her. It'll be worse for everybody all around if you try to hide it."

His face grew agitated and he began rubbing his forehead with short, rapid strokes with two fingers. Finally he let out a sigh of resignation. "I suppose you're right. It would look worse if it came out later, probably worse than it really is." He began chewing his lips, then went on. "Five days ago Farnsworth came to me and said that he thought he might know where Susan was. He said he'd been talking to a former member of the Word of God whom he'd deprogrammed, that the guy thought Sievers might be keeping her at some other retreat the group has somewhere."

"Did he say where this retreat was supposed to be?"

"No. Apparently the person he talked to wasn't sure himself. He'd been shown a photograph of the place, but he'd never been there. Only advanced members got to go there, or something like that."

"So where did the five hundred come in?"

"Farnsworth said he needed it for expenses."

"What happened to the other thousand?"

He shrugged. "He said it went for legal expenses. Farnsworth was having legal problems; a lot of people were suing him for personal damages. That's why he has—had—to charge so much money for his services. He told me he started out just charging people for his expenses, but then the lawsuits started coming in, and he had to up his fees to cover the costs."

"Why didn't you tell me all this before?"

"I don't know," he said, sounding sincere. "I was waiting to hear from Farnsworth. Then when he didn't call, I didn't know what to think. I tried calling him several times, but his line was out of order—"

"That doesn't answer my question."

He looked down at his feet. "You were right. I thought I was doubling my chances by having two of you looking for Susan. I didn't tell you about Farnsworth because I didn't want you to think I didn't have confidence in you. You seem pretty independent-minded. I was afraid you'd quit, and I wanted you on the case."

"Why? We haven't quite established that fact yet."

"I did some checking around before I called you," he said. "You were recommended to me as being one of the most reliable and competent men in your field in Los Angeles."

"By whom?"

"Sam Feldstein, for one."

I nodded. Sam Feldstein was a building contractor who had hired me last year to track down a hundred thousand dollars worth of lumber that had vanished from one of his building sites. I managed to do that, finally locating it wrapped in polyethylene plastic at the bottom of a river near Prescott, Arizona. The fore- man on the building project and two of his assistants were subse- quently arrested and convicted of grand theft. "You know Sam?"

"I used to be his broker," Haynes said, then scowled. "You don't think Susan is involved in any way in this murder thing, do you? I mean, just because Farnsworth was looking for her, that doesn't mean she had anything to do with him getting killed."

I didn't know whether he was asking me or commanding me not to believe. "There's no reason to think she is tied up in any way with it," I said. "Not at this time, anyway."

He gave me a worried nod. "What do you think I should tell the police if they ask me about the money?"

"Just what you told me. The cops have a way of finding things out anyway. If you try giving them a story, you're going to get tripped up on it. Just tell them the truth, with no embellishment."

"What are you going to do?"

"Stay as clear of the Farnsworth murder as I can. As far as I'm concerned, it's a police matter now. They get very touchy about strangers meddling in their cases."

"So where are you going to look?"

"I want to check out this Gypsy character who wrote the letter we found in her room. From what I've learned, it looks like he was one of the bikers she was arrested with last year. Sievers said that the guy was visiting her this summer while she was living at the commune."

"You'd trust Sievers to tell you the truth?"

"His story checks out."

"God, I hope she's not mixed up with that bunch of gutter trash again."

"You really care about her, don't you?"

He nodded and looked down at his hands. "It's a hard thing to explain. I always wanted a kid of my own, but things just didn't work out somehow. My first wife had a miscarriage, and the doctors told her she couldn't have children after that. Our marriage lasted seven years, then things came apart and we got divorced. By the time I'd met Cynthia I was already past the mating age. And then, she already had Susie. I guess Susie is the closest I'll ever come to a daughter of my own."

I stood up. He looked up from the pavement. "You going?"

I nodded. "You're going to tell the cops what you told me about the money, aren't you? Because if they ask me, I'm not going to lie to them about it—"

"Yes, don't worry. I'll tell them."

"Okay. I'll let you know if I turn up anything."

I turned and went through the sliding glass door, into the house. I made it through the living room without seeing a sign of either Mrs. Haynes or Maria and quietly let myself out.

CHAPTER TEN

I had already had one drink and was starting on my second when I saw Al Herrera's stocky form come through the front doors of Luigi's. He stood in the entranceway, scanning the scattered faces in the room. I stood up and raised a hand. He nodded and started across the obstacle course of tables to where I had resumed my seat.

"How long you been here?" he asked, thrusting out a beefy brown hand. My own disappeared in it.

"Not long. Couple of minutes."

He dropped into a chair and pointed at my drink. "I could use one of those." He turned in his chair and signaled to the cocktail waitress—a tall, big-busted redhead dressed in a tightly cinched, abbreviated version of a Sicilian peasant's dress. She was standing at the service area, waiting for a drink order. When she saw Al motioning to her, she nodded and went to another table to deliver her tray full of drinks.

Al turned back around. In the dim light of the room I could still make out the bags under his eyes. "You look tired."

"Yeah, I am." He smiled, but the smile was only an effort. It lasted only a second, then the corners of the mouth dropped into an exhausted frown. "We've had a series of burglary-murders over in the *barrio*—four of them in the past three weeks—and not the usual gang stuff. All of the victims have been old, all of them beaten to death. A goddamn tio-taco city councilman by the name of Alvarez who's trying to prove to his constituents that he's a Mexican has been putting a lot of heat on the department. You know all the bullshit, about how the department only works to solve murders when the victims are white and rich. I've been getting the backwash, working on the cases day and night for the past two weeks, trying to get a lead."

The cocktail waitress came over holding an empty tray, and asked what he would like. Watching Al, I knew what he would like. The fatigue disappeared from his face as he stared admiringly at her breasts which swelled like two pale, ripe melons from the top of her blouse. He ordered a bourbon and soda and continued to stare as she sauntered back to the bar.

"Jesus Christ," he said, finally turning back around. "Did you get a load of those tits? Beautiful."

"Rose would kill you."

"I can look, can't I? You stop looking, buddy, you might as well be dead."

"You have any ideas?"

He smiled. "Plenty."

"About the murders, I mean."

"Plenty of those, too. Plenty of ideas, plenty of fingerprints, but no suspects. We know that there are at least three of them and that they're kids. They're too stupid and too sloppy not to be. On the last job they pulled, all the dumb punks got was a piggy bank. You should have seen the old lady they killed to get it. They smashed in her face and kicked in her ribs, just for a couple of lousy dollars in change."

"I hope you get them."

"We'll get them. Not that it'll make any difference. Some asshole judge will wind up slapping their wrists and packing them off to CYA, and they'll be out in two years, doing the same fucking thing."

His voice was flat and indifferent, but it masked a bitterness that I knew was deep and real. I have found most cops I have run across to be quite vocal when expressing opinions about courts and lenient judges. But I have also found that few of them take their jobs so seriously that they are obsessive about the subject. Al was. Police work was his life, and for the five years or so that I had known him, he had been hemorrhaging internally because of it. Sitting there watching the tired face, I couldn't help but wonder how much more he could bleed before something inside him died and he took the irrevocable step over the line and started wasting suspects to make sure they stayed off the streets.

The cocktail waitress returned with his drink and then wandered off again into the din of clinking glasses and conversation. Al raised his glass in a mock salute and took a swallow. He put

73

the glass back down on the table and reached into his sports coat. He pulled out a small, black notebook and said: "I'd better dictate this. I don't think you'll be able to read my writing."

I got out my own notebook and pen, and he began.

"John Lee Hunter, AKA Gypsy. Caucasian, age 29, five-foot-eleven inches tall, weight 185. Brown hair and eyes, wears his hair long, also a mustache. Identifying marks and scars: a dragon tattooed on the right forearm and a dagger on the left. On the left hand, also, he has a number '8' tattooed between the index finger and thumb, standing for the eighth letter of the alphabet, 'H', meaning 'heroin.' He has a five-inch scar across his chest, the result of a knife fight in the seventh grade. He was born in Valparaiso, Indiana—"

"Valparaiso, Indiana? You've got to be kidding."

He took a sip from his drink and said: "You want to hear this shit or not?"

"Okay, okay. So solly."

"He was one of three sons and daughters born to Mr. and Mrs. Benjamin Hunter. The parents are divorced. The old man is an auto mechanic and still lives in Valparaiso. The mother has been remarried twice since Hunter. She's currently married to one Barry Muller, 531 Altamira Drive, Huntington Park. Hunter lived with them there when he was a kid but didn't get along with Muller. According to the P.O., this Muller drinks a lot and used to beat the shit out of the kids. He even sent Hunter to the hospital once and wound up getting slapped with a felony child-abuse charge.

"Anyway, Hunter's been a chronic runaway since he was ten and was in and out of trouble all his life. Since 1959 he's been arrested seven times—for assault, burglary, carrying a concealed weapon, twice for vagrancy, indecent exposure, and possession. He had been convicted only four times, for the vag, possession, concealed weapon, and indecent exposure charges. Drug history: he's used most of the hallucinogens, pot, reds, and he's chipped heroin, but from what this Weiskopf says, he was never addicted.

"He was released from County Jail on July 12 of this year after serving six months for a possession of marijuana charge and is currently serving three years' probation. His current address is 401 Rosedale Avenue, Apartment 5, in Palms. He's been living there since he got out of the slammer."

74

"What about employment?"

"After he was released from County, he worked for a couple of weeks as a sheet-metal man for a Culver City fabricating firm but was fired for insubordination. That's been the pattern of his life. Presently unemployed."

"I wonder what he's doing for bread?"

"His P.O. says collecting unemployment, but I'd be willing to bet he's got something going on the side, like stripping cars or knocking over liquor stores."

"You're really a cynic."

"When it comes to assholes like this Hunter, you bet your ass I am."

"How often does Hunter report in to his P.O.?"

"Twice a month for urinalysis."

"Did this Weiskopf give you any idea what Hunter is like?"

"Uh-huh. He said Hunter is a sociopathic personality with the standard outlaw hostility to authority figures. He has a tendency to explode, sometimes violently. Hunter even came close to jumping him a couple of times, right there in the office. Apparently all it takes is for somebody to cross the wrong wires."

"If he's so dangerous, why did they let him out on probation?"

He shrugged. "You figure it out. I'm tired of trying." He picked up his drink and paused with it on the way to his lips. "Now, you want to tell Uncle Albert what it's all about?"

I sketched in the case for him, and his homicide-inclined mind displayed some interest when I got to the Farnsworth murder.

"How are you figuring the killing?"

"I'm not. I'm leaving that up to the homicide boys."

"Got any theories?"

"Absolutely none. And that's the way I'm leaving it."

He nodded, eyeing my empty glass. "Another drink?"

"I can't. Got to check out this address of Hunter's yet."

"Okay," he said and reached for the check.

I stretched out my hand and said: "I've got a paying client now. I can afford it."

"The county has more money than your client. Let them pick it up. You're an informer, right? Giving me a tip on a very important case."

"Speaking of tip, the county isn't picking that up. I'll get it."

"Okay," he relented. "You get the tip."

We put our money down on the table and Al ripped the receipt off the bottom of the check, and we walked to the door.

"Where are you parked?" I asked when we got outside.

"Down the street in a red zone."

"You've probably got a ticket by now."

He shrugged. "I'll file it in the glove box with the rest. I've got one of the radio cars."

"I'm right over here," I said, pointing toward my car.

He walked over to it with me and pointed a finger at the gaping dent in the door. "Looks like somebody clobbered you pretty good."

"You know what the bastard did?" I said angrily. "He hit me while I was parked and left a note on my windshield saying: 'I just backed into your car. There's a crowd watching me and they think I'm writing down my name and address, but I'm not.'"

"That's an old joke," he said, laughing anyway.

"When I find the son of a bitch, he won't think it's so funny."

"How are you going to find him? You got a witness?"

"No, but I've got paint scrapings from his car. I'm currently in the process of tracking down all the blue cars in the city. I figure I should have them all checked out by 1989."

"Well, good luck, buddy."

"Thanks, I'll need it."

We said our good-byes and I thanked him for the drinks and he turned and walked down the street. I unlocked the car door and got in. He was bent over the hood of his car as I drove past and honked. He looked up and waved, the yellow parking ticket flying like a pennant from his fist.

CHAPTER ELEVEN

Rosedale Drive ran off Overland for about three blocks before it jagged to the right and changed names. Most of the three blocks was occupied by new, 200-unit apartment complexes with pseudo-Spanish exteriors and names like Casa Dorado or Villa Hermosa or Vista del Sol, but there were a few older and smaller apartment buildings strung out along the street, stubbornly clinging to their sections of turf, trying to hold their ground against the invasion of the new giants. One of these was 401. It looked like it was losing the battle.

It was a two-story, white building with some sick-looking banana plants growing in brick planters out front. It was in desperate need of a paint job. Red-brown rust stains ran down its sides in tapering trails from the bottom of its window screens. There was a sign stuck in the small patch of weedy lawn out front that read: FOR RENT—ONE BEDRM. APT. INQUIRE APT. #1—MGR.

Number five was on the ground floor away from the street, at the end of a long, cracked concrete walk. I knocked on the door, got no response, and knocked again. After waiting a couple more seconds, I went back down the walk to the mailboxes. The name slot above number five was blank. Apartment one was right by the mailboxes and I stepped over and knocked on its door.

A small, bird-like woman with tiny black eyes and a beakish nose answered the door. She looked at me petulantly, as if she were going to peck me for disturbing her, and said: "Yes?"

Even her voice was bird-like, high-pitched and twittering. From behind her, a monotonic male voice droned out the five o'clock news from a hidden television set.

"I'd like to speak to the manager."

"I'm the manager. Mrs. Coates is the name."

"I was wondering if you could give me some information about apartment five?"

Her expression softened as she smiled hopefully. "Are you looking for an apartment?"

"Not really," I said, digging out my wallet. "My name is Asch, Mrs. Coates. I'm a private detective, looking for John Lee Hunter. The last address I have for him is 401 Rosedale Drive, Apartment five."

I held up my license and she took the wallet out of my hand, squinting at it in the fading daylight. She handed it back and said in an annoyed tone: "Well, he doesn't live here anymore, so you can go look elsewhere. He moved out bag and baggage five days ago."

"Did he leave any forwarding address?"

"No, he didn't. As a matter of fact, he left in the middle of the night, owing me two weeks rent." She stopped and turned her head slightly to one side, squinting at me through one eye. "What are you after him for?"

"I'm not, exactly. I'm looking for a girl who might be with him. She ran away from home a few days ago. I'm working for her parents."

"The little one with the frizzy blond hair?"

"You've seen her?"

"If it's the same one," she said. "She came here with Hunter the day he ran out on the rent."

"I have a photograph of the girl I'm looking for in my car, Mrs. Coates. If I showed it to you, do you think you would be able to tell me if it was the same girl who was here with Hunter?"

Her narrow shoulders hunched up in a nervous shrug and she put a freckled hand to her throat. "I suppose so."

"I'll be right back," I said and bounded down the front steps. I picked up the manila envelope containing Susan's graduation picture off the seat and went back up the walk to where Mrs. Coates was standing. I unsheathed the picture from the envelope and handed it to her.

She tapped it twice with an index finger and nodded. "That's her. She was the one with Hunter."

She pushed the picture aggressively back at me. I took it and slipped it back in its envelope. "You're a fantastic witness, Mrs. Coates," I said in an attempt to break through her sullen crust.

78

"Thank you. Your identification is the most important lead I've gotten so far."

She seemed to respond to the compliment. Her mouth lost some of its petulance and she nodded thoughtfully. "It's my business to notice what goes on around here. Harold and I—Harold's my husband—Harold and I have managed these apartments for nine years now, and we've never had a complaint from the owners yet. That's because we notice what goes on."

"I bet you watch them as if they were your own."

The thawing process was complete. She smiled. "We do. If you ask me, that's the trouble with people today. Nobody has any sense of responsibility anymore."

"You're absolutely right," I said. "Would you mind if I asked you some questions, Mrs. Coates?"

"I guess it would be all right. You might as well come in and be comfortable. It's getting kind of chilly out here."

The living room was small and stuffy. I sat down on a plaid couch and Mrs. Coates went over to the television set and turned down the volume. Then she sat down in a chair on the other side of a maple coffee table. She sat rigidly, with her back and neck stiffly upright.

"What day did you say the girl was here?" I asked.

"Five days ago. Monday. I was outside, doing some watering, and they came riding in on his motorcycle—"

"The girl and Hunter?"

"Yes. I noticed her because she looked so young. I knew she couldn't have been a day past sixteen and I said to myself: 'That girl belongs in school, not riding around on the back of some hoodlum's motorcycle.'"

I could have told her that she was off by two years but didn't. She was starting to talk now, and I didn't want to do anything that might stop the flow. "Her parents couldn't agree with you more. Did you say anything to either of them at the time?"

"As a matter of fact, I did. Hunter was two weeks behind in his rent, like I said, and I reminded him about it. He got real nasty about it—started using four-letter words like they were going out of style—and he and the girl went storming into his apartment. Well, that was the last straw. We'd had trouble with Hunter before. He'd only lived here a couple of months, but we'd had to warn him a few times about playing loud music late at night and having those friends of his around here, drinking beer and raising all kinds of hell, frightening the other tenants. We've got a nice clientele here, you know, not fancy people or anything like that, but decent, working people. We weren't about to lose any of them for the likes of Hunter. But up to Monday, he'd always quieted down when we'd asked him to. When he started calling me those names, though, that was the last straw. I told Harold when he got home from work—he works for a plumbing contractor—I said I didn't have to take abuse from that kind of trash and I wanted him out of here."

She paused, and I said: "What did Harold say to that?"

"He said he would go down and get an eviction notice the next day. He was kind of nervous about it. He thought Hunter was going to try to make some trouble about it, but I told him flat out, either Hunter goes or I do." She thrust out her jaw belligerently, as if ready to do battle with the ghost of her husband's cowardice. "Anyway, it turned out all of Harold's worrying was for nothing."

"Why?"

"I told you. Hunter packed up and left in the middle of the night, just like some sneak thief. Left the door of the apartment wide open, too. We discovered it the next morning. Anybody could have come in there during the night and carted off anything they wanted—"

"Was the girl with him when he left?"

"I wouldn't know. I didn't see either of them leave."

"Mrs. Coates, do you think it would be possible for me to look around the apartment?"

She bit her lip and held it and cocked her head to one side. "Well, I don't know—"

"It might be very important. For the girl's sake. She has serious emotional problems and her parents are worried sick about her."

"They must be rich to be able to hire private detectives to go traipsing around looking for their daughter."

Her tone was beginning to take on a petulant edge again. I tried to head it off. "They're not. But they are willing to spend their last quarter to find her. She's all they've got." I let that sink in and asked: "Do you have any children of your own, Mrs. Coates?"

"We have a son," she said proudly. "He'll be graduating from college next year. San Francisco State."

"Then you must know what this girl's parents are going through."

She thought about it for a few seconds and said: "I don't suppose it would hurt anything. After all, the place is vacant."

She got up and disappeared through a hallway. When she returned, she was holding a set of keys. We left her apartment and went down the walk to number five.

"You'll have to excuse the way the place looks," she said, as if forgetting I wasn't a prospective tenant. "It's not completely cleaned up yet. Hunter really left things in a mess. We had to replace some of the furniture he and his friends broke up." She inserted the key into the door handle and pushed the door open. She went in first and ran a hand along the wall, feeling for the light switch. She found it, and the dark room came alive with light.

The floor plan was basically the same as the apartment I had just left, but the graying carpet was more soiled and threadbare, and the furniture was cheaper—vinyl and pressed wood.

"Have you vacuumed the place yet?"

"Yes," she said. "Yesterday."

"Did you empty the wastebaskets?"

"Sure."

I gave a disappointed nod and started going over the room. I checked underneath the couch and chairs and then removed the vinyl cushions from them. I pushed a hand down in the crack between the backs and the seats, checking for anything that might have dropped out of Hunter's pockets while he was sitting down. I came up with a paper clip, a ball-point pen, and some lint.

"What are you looking for?" Mrs. Coates asked.

"I don't know," I said and put the cushions back on the couch.

I went into the kitchen and opened the drawers. Some assorted kitchen utensils, a few odd pieces of stainless steel tableware. A can of fruit cocktail and two cans of pork and beans were the only inhabitants of the cupboards above the stove. I opened the cupboard underneath the sink and checked the wastebasket there, just to make sure Mrs. Coates hadn't missed anything. She hadn't.

I went back to the living room and pointed down a hallway that ran off to my left. "The bedroom in there?"

"Yes."

I went down the hallway and turned on the lights in the bedroom. It was a tiny, bare-walled box, with one curtained window that looked out onto the trash area out back. Aside from the bed, which was stripped down to the stained mattress, the only furniture in the room was a flimsy, blond dresser, the top of which was covered with cigarette burns. After going through the dresser, I lifted up the mattress and looked under it, then opened the sliding door of the closet. It was empty, except for a half-dozen wire hangers and a couple of pillows stashed away on the shelf. I slid the door shut and went down the hall to the bathroom, with Mrs. Coates trailing behind me.

The bathroom looked cleaner than the rest of the place. I guessed that Mrs. Coates had already been in there with her sponge and cleanser. The sink and shower had a scrubbed, disinfected look, and the medicine cabinet was empty and spotless.

"Well," I said, the disappointment apparent in my voice. "I guess that's it."

"You find anything?"

"No, but thanks for letting me look."

"If I would have known, I wouldn't have cleaned the place. But I didn't know."

I followed her out into the living room, and she turned out the lights and pulled the door shut. At her door, I said good-bye and left her one of my cards in case she heard anything from Hunter, then went down the walk to my car.

The smell of barbecueing steaks and the sound of laughter and people swimming drifted through the wrought iron gates of the rough-plaster apartment complex across the street. I wished I was with them. I pulled away from the curb and made a U-turn toward Overland.

CHAPTER TWELVE

The house was a small, peeling tract home that shared a treeless block with other small, peeling tract houses that looked just like it. I went across the small patch of dry lawn, past the almost-new pickup truck and the beat-up Falcon station wagon that sat in the driveway, to the front door. I pressed the bell and heard a man's voice yell over the volume of the television set that was blaring sirens and gunfire. "Somebody's at the door!"

Another voice shouted something from farther back in the house, and the man's voice yelled back: "I'm watching a program, goddamn it!"

I waited for them to make up their minds which one was going to go for the door. Then the naked bug light above the door switched on, bathing the front porch in yellow light, and the door opened.

The man who opened it was big and heavyset, with wide shoulders and a beer belly that hung over the top of his gray work pants. He had dark, wavy hair and a wide nose and a large, fleshy mouth that seemed to be set in a permanent sneer. "Yeah?" he asked crossly.

"You Barry Muller?"

"What if I am?"

"My name is Asch," I said, taking a card out of my wallet and handing it to him. "I'd like to talk to you and your wife, if you wouldn't mind."

He took a step outside the door and took the card, his face turning jaundiced in the yellow light. "Private detective? What do you want to talk to us about?"

"I'm looking for John Hunter."

"Yeah? What did the punk do now?"

"Nothing that I know of," I said. "He was a witness to a traffic accident a few months back. I'm working for an attorney who is representing the man who was hit. John's testimony could be important to our case."

"Well, he's not here," he said flatly. "He ain't been around here in a couple of months."

"Have any idea where I might find him?"

Before he could answer, a small, tired-looking woman appeared in the doorway behind him, wiping her hands nervously on her waist apron. She had a pale, puffy face in which small, dark eyes were set like two raisins in cookie dough. She wore a silver wig on her head and a few strands of telltale dark hair peeped out from the edges of it. She looked at me worriedly and said: "What is it? I heard something about John. Is he in trouble?"

Muller whirled around and said sharply: "He's always in trouble, that no-good punk son of yours. That's all he's ever been—trouble."

I looked past Muller at the woman and forced a smile. "You're John's mother, I take it."

"Yes," she said, nodding weakly.

"My name is Asch, Mrs. Muller. I'm a private detective. I was just explaining to your husband that there is no trouble. I'm only looking for John because he was a witness to a traffic accident a couple of months ago in which a man was seriously injured. I'm working for the attorney who is handling the man's case and we're trying to get in touch with John to get a deposition from him as to what he saw."

"I haven't seen John," she said. "He doesn't come here much."

"I appreciate that," I said. "But it's very important that we get in touch with him. His testimony could be very important to our client's case. And of course, there would be a substantial witness fee for John if he would come down and give us a deposition."

Muller turned back to me, his face lighted with interest. "What kind of witness fee?"

"Normally, Mr. Muller, fees are paid to witnesses in civil cases like this, as remuneration for the inconvenience and expense of having to take time off work to give testimony, but since the amount of money involved in this case is so great, the attorney I'm working for has authorized me to pay John $200 just to come

84

down to his office and give a statement. He doesn't even have to appear in court."

"Two hundred bucks?" he said. Thoughts moved visibly behind his eyes. "That's a good chunk of bread. How much is this guy who got hit trying to settle for?"

"Half a million."

He whistled softly. "What the hell happened to him? He lose an arm or something?"

"He's paralyzed from the waist down."

"Gee, that's tough," he said, the veneer of concern that covered his voice sounding paper-thin.

"I have also been authorized by my employer to offer a cash finder's fee to anyone who might be able to help us locate John and persuade him to come down to the office—"

His wife started shaking her head and said: "We don't have—"

"Shut up," Muller said, snapping his head around toward her. "I'll handle this." Then to me again: "What kind of a finder's fee?"

"May I come in?"

He thought about it and then flashed me a friendly smile. "Sure. Come in."

I stepped into a boxy, plasterboard living room cluttered with furniture that looked as if it had been beaten into submission by years of abuse. The room smelled of cigarette smoke and whiskey and on the coffee table in front of the couch were the sources of both the odors. A fifth of cheap bourbon and a glass with some half-melted ice cubes in its bottom sat on the table, next to an ashtray filled with cigarette butts.

"Sit down," Muller said.

I sat in a lumpy chair. Muller went over to the TV and switched off the cops-and-robbers program I had heard from the door. He came back over and sat on the couch. His wife sat on the edge of another chair, farther away.

"Have a drink?" Muller asked, motioning to the bottle on the table.

"No, thanks," I said. "But I could sure use a cup of coffee, if you've got one around." I didn't really want a cup of coffee, just Mrs. Muller out of the room. I had a feeling that she was going to be a drag to the negotiations to come.

"Sure, we've got some coffee," he said, smiling. "Clarice, go and get Mr. Asch a cup of coffee. And bring me some more ice."

He picked up his glass and held it out to her. She reluctantly got out of her chair and took it. She gave me a worried look, but I smiled assuringly; she returned the smile and left the room.

"I always have a drink when I get home from work," he said self-consciously as he watched her go. "Helps me unwind."

I nodded and said: "What kind of work do you do, Mr. Muller?"

"I work for the Gardner Outdoor Advertising Company. We make billboards."

"That sounds like an interesting business," I lied.

He shrugged. "It's all right. The pay is pretty good. Four-seventy-five an hour."

"That's pretty good pay."

"It's all right," he said. "But a little something extra never hurt, either, if you get what I mean." He smiled, then leaned forward on the couch. "You said something about a finder's fee. What kind of fee you talking about?"

"Fifty dollars. Twenty in advance, the other thirty when I get in touch with Hunter."

"If this case is worth half a million bucks, it should be worth more than fifty lousy bucks to find your star witness."

I stared at him blankly. "Fifty dollars is all I'm authorized to offer."

He licked his lips and leaned back again seemingly immersed in thought. He turned toward the kitchen door and yelled: "Clarice, where's my ice, goddamn it?!"

The door opened and his wife came out, holding the glass full of fresh cubes. She handed it to him, then turned to me: "What do you want in your coffee?"

"Cream and one sugar, please."

She gave me a tired nod. "It's instant. I hope you don't mind. That's all I got."

"That's fine."

"The kettle's on now. It'll be ready in just a second."

"Thank you," I said.

"When's dinner going to be ready?" Muller asked her, his voice sharp.

"I'm waiting for the kids to get home."

"To hell with them," Muller said. "They know what time dinner is around here. If they don't want to eat, it's their tough luck. I'm hungry."

"I didn't mean to interrupt your dinner," I said, trying to sound apologetic.

"That's okay," he said, motioning for me to stay put even though I hadn't moved. "Go get that coffee, Clarice."

She went through the kitchen door again. Muller filled his glass with bourbon and sat back comfortably on the couch, sipping it.

"How many children do you have, Mr. Muller?" I asked, just to be making conversation.

"Two. Two boys."

"How old are they?"

"Sixteen and seventeen."

"They live at home?"

He nodded.

"They're not home now, I take it."

"No," he said, his voice acquiring a hard edge. "But they should be. I don't know about these kids today. They wander around the goddamn streets until all hours. If I was ever late for dinner like they are all the time, my father would have beat the holy shit out of me. These kids today, they get away with murder. They got no respect for their parents or anybody else. They must learn all this shit in school, from these goddamn hippie schoolteachers. You ever see some of these schoolteachers today? Long hair and beards, always spouting off about freedom and all that shit. They shouldn't be allowed to teach, those bastards. They're poisoning the kids' minds."

I felt like telling Muller that he should look closer to home for the reasons his children were going sour on him. "John is your stepson, is that right?"

"Yeah, that's right."

"What's he like?"

"He's a smart-mouthed punk," he said. "And the other two are just like him."

"You mean your two children?"

He waved the hand holding the drink, nearly spilling some of the bourbon in the process. "No, her two kids. She's got two others, a boy and a girl. They're all from the same rotten barrel."

"Do they live here?"

"No, thank God. They all moved out. And good riddance, too. They sponged off me long enough."

"Where are they now?"

He shrugged indifferently. "I don't know. The girl got pregnant and married some guy up in San Francisco, the last I heard. The other brother, Rich, he dropped out of high school a couple of years ago and took off. He's probably in jail somewhere by now. I tried to set them right, but none of them listened to me. They were already rotten by the time I married Clarice. It was too late to teach them anything. Especially that John. He was the worst of the bunch—"

"That's not true," Mrs. Muller said from the door of the kitchen. She was holding a cup and saucer and started forward with it. She handed it to me, and I thanked her. She said: "John is a good boy. Really. He and Barry never got along, that's all. He's a hard boy to understand. He always was—"

"Hard to understand, shit," Muller interrupted her. "He's a punk. What's so hard to understand about that?"

"He never had a chance—"

"Chance, hell," he said disgustedly. "I'm sick of hearing about this 'chance' stuff. He had all the chances anybody else did." His wife's defense of her son seemed to evoke a catalytic response in him. He leaned forward intensely and said: "Go get John's address."

"How do we know he's telling the truth?" she said to him, purposely avoiding eye contact with me. "How do we know he isn't some bill collector or something?"

"Don't be ridiculous. That worthless son of a bitch couldn't owe that much money that a bill collector would be willing to pay fifty bucks to just get in contact with him. Now get that goddamn address—"

"Can I talk to you a minute, alone?" she asked.

His wide face reddened, and he got up out of his seat. "I'll be right back," he said to me, then went out with her to the kitchen. Their voices drifted back out to me through the closed door, muffled and indistinguishable at first, then picking up volume.

"—John might not like it."

"I don't give a shit what John likes. You got to be crazy to think I'm going to throw away fifty bucks because he might not like it."

"I don't know—"

His voice lowered into a menacing growl, and he said: "You don't get me, Clarice. I'm not asking you. I'm telling you. Get that address. Now."

There was a silence after that, and he came walking back out through the door, holding an address book and smiling. "Here it is. He lives at 521 Rosedale Avenue, Apartment 5, in Palms."

"Lived," I said. "He moved out of there several days ago without leaving a forwarding address. That's what I came over here for. I thought he might have told you where he was moving."

That stopped him. The smile vanished and his face reddened again. He shouted over his shoulder toward the door: "Clarice!"

Mrs. Muller came through the doorway looking defeated. I felt a twinge of guilt that I was adding to the burden of life that she was already carrying but buried that thought by focusing my attention on what I had come for.

"He's not living at this address anymore," Muller said angrily.

"So?" she asked timidly. "What do you want me to do about it? I haven't seen him in months. If he's not there, I don't know where he is."

"You're sure he didn't call you and tell you he was moving?" Muller asked, taking a step toward her.

She took a frightened step back and said: "Sure I'm sure."

"What's the name of that bike shop he's always hanging around over in Culver City? He left you that number one time, when Rich was in the hospital."

She shook her silver wig and said: "I don't remember. I wrote it down. It's in the book."

He sat down on the couch and started thumbing through the pages of the book, until he stopped with his finger on one page. "Here it is. Skip's Chop Shop. 426–1312."

I jotted down the name and number in my notebook. As I was writing, he said: "Somebody there'll know where he is. That whole bunch of his hangs out there."

"I'll check it out," I said. "Thanks."

"How about the twenty?"

I took a twenty out of my wallet and handed it to him, then marked down on my "Expenses" page, $20—informant's fee—B. Muller.

Muller jammed the twenty into his pants pocket and said eagerly: "When did you say I get the other thirty?"

"When I get in touch with John."

"How am I going to know when that happens?"

"I'll let you know, don't worry."

He looked at me suspiciously but said nothing. I put the coffee cup down on the table and stood up. "I guess that should do it. Thanks for the coffee, Mrs. Muller. If you happen to hear from John, tell him I was by looking for him and ask him to get in touch with me. My number is on the card there."

I felt a sudden release as I stepped outside into the night air, out of the thick tension in the house. I took a deep breath and started across the lawn to the car, but stopped dead when I heard shots ring out from inside the house. I turned but then heard the sirens and the screeching tires and the changing of channels. I turned back and went down to the street.

CHAPTER THIRTEEN

I took Slauson over to Culver City. Skip's Chop Shop was located on a dingy block of Jefferson Boulevard, a small, gray, cement brick box with double aluminum garage doors across its front. One of the doors was open as I passed, and I got a glimpse of people inside. I drove up the block and parked and walked back.

The people I had seen turned out to be three rancid-looking Satan's Warriors who were sitting on the seats of their chopped and raked hogs, shooting the breeze and guzzling cans of Coors.

Their hair was long and matted, and their hands were blackened by an accumulation of grease and dirt. All were bearded and all wore the same costume: grease-encrusted blue jeans and motorcycle boots, T-shirts that might have once been white but which had darkened to a dull, gray-brown, and sleeveless jean jackets that looked as if they had been dipped in crankcase oil and set out in the sun to dry. Each of them was flying the club's patch on his jacket—a bat-winged demon riding a chopped hog, the words "Satan's Warriors, Culver City," in blood-red letters underneath.

Sitting on the sleek, gleaming, immaculately chromed machines, they looked almost comical, like some trained, lice-ridden animal act, ready to kick over their motors and roar across the stage on cue from their absentee, tuxedoed trainer.

As I stepped into the light the conversation stopped and the three heads turned to look at me. A fourth man, this one jacketless, was sitting in the corner on the oil-stained cement floor, tinkering with the engine of a purple-flamed Harley 74. He looked up when he heard the talking stop, saw me, and stood up, wiping his hands on an orange rag.

"Can I help you with something?" he asked.

He was short and slightly built and looked older than the

others, maybe 30 or so. His eyes were yellow-green, the color of a wolf's eyes, and his clean-shaven face was lean and predatory.

I stepped past the others and said: "That depends. You Skip?"

"Yeah, I'm Skip."

"I thought maybe you could tell me where I might be able to find John Lee Hunter."

He tried on his puzzled look. Maybe he was the world's greatest motorcycle mechanic, but he was a lousy actor. "Who?"

"Gypsy."

"Sorry, I don't know any Gypsy."

"He rides with the Satan's Warriors. I thought for sure you'd know him."

He shook his head. "These guys are Warriors. Maybe they can help you. You dudes know a Warrior named Gypsy?"

They all put on their most puzzled looks. "Gypsy?" one of them said. "Never heard of anybody by that name. You guys know anybody by that name?"

They shook their heads, and Skip turned to me and shrugged. "Nobody knows any Gypsy. Sorry. What are you looking for him for?"

"It's a personal matter."

One of them stuck his nose up in the air and took a noisy whiff. "I smell a pig."

"You a pig, mister?" Skip asked.

"Private detective," I said. I took a card out of my wallet and handed it to him. "Look, I'm not looking for Gypsy to make any trouble for him. I just want to talk to him about somebody he knows, that's all. If and when he happens to come by, I'd appreciate it if you'd give him this card. He can call me anytime. I just want to talk to him."

He scrutinized the card, then put it away in his pocket. "Okay, now you can vacate the premises, man."

"Sure," I said and started out of the garage.

I was stopped by a booted foot which was shoved across my path. The burly, bearded gorilla who belonged to the foot looked up at me from the seat of his chopper and smiled, exposing a mouthful of rotten teeth. His thick arms were folded belligerently across his chest. Tattooed on one well-muscled forearm was a blue dagger and the words "Born to Lose." I didn't especially want to be the one to determine whether or not the tattoo was prophecy.

"Hey, dude," he said, "are you as slick as all those private eyes I seen in the movies?"

He looked over at the others. They were all smiling as if they had seen his act before and were anticipating what was coming next. "I bet you carry a snub-nose .38 in a shoulder holster under that coat, right? You run across a bad hombre and whip it out and drop him at a hundred yards—slicker than shit—POW! Right?" He reached inside his jean jacket and pulled out an index finger and pointed it at me, his thumb working the hammer of the make-believe gun.

One of the others guffawed. The one with the imaginary gun looked over at him and smiled, then turned back to me. "How about it, dude? You as slick as all that? You get all that fine-looking pussy crawling all over you, just begging for a fuck, like I seen in the movies?"

The decayed smile was frozen on his face now. He leaned forward, tense, waiting for a word, anything, that would give him an excuse to come down on me, but I wasn't about to give him one. I knew that the second he swung, the others would be up and into it, and I had weak kidneys anyway. Their condition couldn't possibly be improved by being stomped by four pairs of heavy boots.

I smiled back at him and stepped over his foot. He waited until I had one leg over and was straddling the foot, then he scissored his legs together, catching my other foot between his. I came down hard. The palms of my hands stung as they hit the cement floor. The fear of getting caught on the ground spurted through me. I rolled over quickly and got back on my feet.

None of them had made a move. They all just sat there, laughing. All except the one who had tripped me. He was still leaning forward in a semi-crouch, his eyes shining in the light like two steel marbles, challenging me to do something—take a step, raise a hand a quarter of an inch.

I was seething inside from a combination of fear and anger and hatred and humiliation. I was afraid to say anything, afraid my voice would crack, so I turned and walked out of the garage.

The three Warriors got off their bikes and followed me outside. They kept about five or six paces behind me, maintaining a steady stream of talk and laughter, telling each other loudly that private eyes weren't at all like they were in the movies, that they were nothing but chickenshit motherfuckers, not worth the toilet paper they used to wipe their asses. They watched from the curb as I unlocked the car door and got behind the steering wheel. For the few seconds it took me to put the key in the ignition and turn over the engine, I thought that was going to be it. But then "Born to Lose," stepped into the gutter and folded his arms again, grinning his death's head grin into my headlights.

I waited for a few seconds, anger boiling up in me again. When it became apparent that he was not going to move, I rolled down my window. "You want to move, please?"

"You want me to move, dude? Move me."

I started inching the car forward, and he took a step back and smashed the heel of his boot into the right headlight. The sound of the shattering glass synchronized with the sound of something shattering in my head. Images raced through my mind: the laughter, the taunts, the foot blocking my path, myself on the ground. Raw anger broke loose in a torrent and flooded through my body.

I jammed the accelerator to the floor. The rotten grin disappeared, and his mouth dropped open to scream. But the scream was drowned out by the squealing of tires. He leaped straight up in the air, arms outstretched, up over the bumper, and landed with a crash on the hood of the car. I punched it out into traffic. Out of the corner of my eye, I saw the other two running down the sidewalk after us. I heard them yelling, but my attention was focused on the face staring at me through the windshield, shouting for me to stop. I accelerated to fifty and jerked the wheel back and forth, sadistically savoring the abject terror in the face as the car swayed from side to side.

I took the next right keeping my foot on it all the way. The tires screamed in protest, and the rear end went into a drift, but I turned the wheel into it, and the car righted itself, and we went charging down the block. I saw the dip before I hit it, but only just before. The car went sailing over it and bottomed out, sparks showering up from the front bumper as it struck the asphalt street. The biker flew up in the air again and came back down on the hood, but his hands maintained their desperate grip on my windshield wipers. I took the next right and his body twisted with the inertia. There was a metallic snap, and the wipers came off in his hands. He rolled off the hood and hit the pavement and I just caught a glimpse of him doing somersaults toward the curb.

I floored it up the street for about three blocks, then turned right again. I stopped at the next corner and scanned the street for any signs of the other two bikers. When I didn't see any, I pulled into traffic and drove up to the freeway. I made a left onto the on-ramp and drove like a madman to the next exit.

CHAPTER FOURTEEN

I got off at 20th, keeping my eyes on the rearview mirror, watching for single headlights, but it was clear. Glancing down at my speedometer, I realized I was speeding and eased up on the gas. I was perspiring freely. The cold air blowing in through the window made me suddenly aware that I was shivering. Rolling up the window and turning on the heat didn't help. I kept on shivering.

When I reached Santa Monica Boulevard I made a right and drove to the first blazing neon sign that said LIQUOR. I parked and went in and bought a half-pint of Jim Beam, then continued down Santa Monica for half a dozen blocks and made a right.

The street I was on was a narrow, residential street lined with small, Spanish-style houses. I parked between street lamps and pulled the half-pint out of its brown paper bag. I unscrewed the top and took a slug from the bottle. The bourbon burned all the way down to my empty stomach and I began to relax almost immediately.

I took another drink and leaned back and closed my eyes, calmly watching the series of broken images that were being replayed on some interior screen in my head. I tried to steer my thoughts away from it, but I involuntarily kept reliving the last 20 minutes, and my eyes snapped open. I thought about my own feelings at the time and wondered what would have happened if the biker's reactions had been a little slower. I tried telling myself that I would have hit my brakes before he went under the tires, but that one would not take. Then I tried telling myself that I had *known* that he would be quick enough to get out of the way, but that would not settle comfortably either.

After another burning swallow of Jim Beam, I was forced to face the fact that at the time I had hit the accelerator, I had been totally consumed by rage. I had not cared whether I killed the man or not. I would have killed him for tripping me. And for kicking in my headlight. Assault and malicious mischief in Jacob Asch's Book of Retribution gets the death penalty. I laughed for no reason at all and took another drink.

You've been on the street too long, Asch, I thought to myself. You've been wading through the shit and the piss and the vomit too goddamn long and you're sinking. . . .

I was getting plastered, there was no doubt about that. I held the bottle up to the light and looked at it. It was about half empty. If I finished it, I knew I would be paralyzed, and although that street was a very nice street, I could think of other places I would rather sleep than in my car.

I put the bottle back into its paper sack, got out of the car, and deposited it in the trunk. I turned around in somebody's driveway and drove back toward Santa Monica, deciding I had better get something to eat.

I drove down the boulevard three blocks and turned into the driveway of Emilio's. The red-jacketed parking attendant looked me and my car over and handed me a ticket with sorrowful disapproval. I went inside.

The restaurant was dimly lit, filled with the faint tinklings of a piano bar and cocktail glasses and the meaningless drone of a hundred mingled conversations. I told the maître d' that I wanted a table for one. He gave me a tight little smile and looked down at his reservation book. He looked back up and told me it would be 20 minutes. If I would care to wait in the bar, he said, he would call me.

I looked at the room. It was nearly a quarter empty, and I told him so. He shrugged indifferently and repeated that it would be 20 minutes. I thought about asking him to step outside in the parking lot where I could run him over and laughed out loud. He looked at me as if I had just escaped from Camarillo. I gave him my name and told him I would be in the bar.

The bar action was kind of slow, and there were only three or four tables filled. The piano player, a middle-aged man with a pencil-thin, Don Ameche mustache, was seated at the grand in the middle of the room, plunking out a slow, jazzy version of "Girl Talk." Nobody seemed to be paying attention. The couples at the tables were absorbed in conversations, and the scattered few at the bar silently absorbed in their own thoughts. I ordered a bourbon and soda from the bartender who was wiping out glasses with a rag.

I looked down the bar at my compatriots, and my eyes stopped on the girl. She was a honey blond in her late twenties, wearing a tight sweater that swelled softly over the curve of her large, rounded breasts which my eyes involuntarily fixed on. I felt the lust rising up slowly, steadily inside, filling my gut.

The bartender brought my drink over and put a check down next to it on the bar. I took a sip from the glass, still staring at the girl. She kept her eyes on her glass which she rotated slowly on the bar top between two long-nailed fingers, seemingly unaware that I was staring at her.

I tried to analyze the source of my lust but was unable to pinpoint it. Maybe it was a holdover from the fear of getting stomped to death I had felt earlier, the animalistic urge to procreate in order to insure the survival of the species.

I finished my drink and ordered another one, thinking about what day it was. Tuesday. Tuesday was Marsha's night off. I put a dollar down on the bar and asked the bartender for change and directions to the pay phone. He pointed toward the front entrance.

Marsha was a 25-year-old cocktail waitress with raven hair and a body that wouldn't quit. She was a cocktail waitress at a supper club on Wilshire called the Old Mariner. She and I had had a thing going for a couple of months, until three weeks ago, when her ex-boyfriend, a bartender who also worked at the Mariner, snowed her into believing that he was through playing around. Marsha had decided to hang us up for awhile, to see what was going to happen between her and her bartender. I had readily assented to the break-up, not feeling any real sense of great loss. But right now, I *was* feeling a great loss.

I dropped my dime and dialed her number, feeling an excited anticipation at hearing her voice again.

"Hello?"

"Hello, Marsha?"

"Yes?" the voice said uncertainly. "Who's this?"

"Jake."

"Oh, hi—" she said, her voice rising as if she intended to go on, but she cut herself off.

98

"How have you been?"

"Fine."

"Can you talk?"

"Uh, not really."

"Is somebody with you?"

"Yeah."

"Oh. I was just calling to find out how things are going with you and your boyfriend."

"Fine, just fine."

"Is that who's there with you now?"

There was a hesitation. "Yes."

I felt a wave of disappointment pass over me. "Well, I won't keep you any longer, then. I was just wondering how you were doing."

"Fine," she said, the voice sounding strained.

"I'll see you then, Marsha."

I hung up the phone and went back to the bar. I downed my drink and ordered another one. I paid for that one and sat brooding over it. The piano player was now working on an upbeat rendition of "When I Fall in Love." I listened for awhile, admiring his use of the keyboard. My eyes drifted automatically down to the blond at the end of the bar. There were two stools between her and the men on either side of her and nobody was making any moves toward her. I was toying with the idea when she looked up from her drink and caught me staring at her. I smiled, but she didn't. She just looked away and took another sip of her drink.

What the hell, I thought, it's worth a try, and got up. I picked up my drink and went down the bar to where she was sitting.

"You mind if I sit here?" I asked, flashing her a million-dollar smile.

She looked up at me with alcoholic blue eyes, and her upper lip curled up as if she were going to hiss. Instead, she merely shrugged indifferently and said: " 's a free country."

I sat down and waited a few seconds before asking her the profound question: "You come here often?"

It wasn't much of a line. Just something to break the ice. She lifted her drink to her lips and held it there, staring straight ahead.

"You come here often?" I asked again.

She turned a cold glare on me and snarled: "Look, you asked if you could sit here, not if you could try to make me."

"I was just trying to be friendly," I said, trying to regain some of my lost ground.

"Friendly, shit," she said, almost shouting. "You're on the goddamn make, like every other asshole man in this town. A girl can't go anywhere without having some jerk trying to hustle her. Well, I'm not here to be hustled, jerk, so if you're going to sit there, shut up."

She whirled furiously around on her stool and took a long belt from her drink. Then she asked the bartender in a loud voice for another.

The man sitting one bar stool down chortled. I sat there for a few seconds too stunned to say anything, then got up and went back to my old spot at the bar, feeling as if I had just taken an ice-cold shower.

The maître d' came into the bar a few minutes later and told me my table was ready. I followed him to a small table in the corner of the dining room where he deposited me with a menu. When the waiter arrived, I ordered another drink, and for dinner, a filet medium rare with a baked potato and a salad with Roquefort.

I took out my frustrated sexual desires on the food and ate ravenously. The dining room was nearly empty by the time I finished my second cup of coffee. I asked the waiter to bring the check. The check was more sobering than the coffee. I paid it and went outside to the parking lot.

A roomful of stuffy, stale air greeted me when I opened my apartment door. I opened the window to get some ventilation into the room and started to undress. That took awhile. Every time I looked down at the buttons of my shirt, I began to sway uncontrollably and had to look up. I had finally finished with the shirt and started on the pants when the phone rang. I picked it up.

"Mr. Asch?"

The voice was soft and female. For some unaccountable reason it flashed through my mind that it was the blond from the bar, calling to apologize for her abominable behavior and to invite me over to her place to go to bed with her. That illusion, as bizarre as it was, was dispelled when the voice said: "This is the answering service, Mr. Asch. I realize it's late, but I've been try-ing to reach you for the past hour. A message came in awhile ago that I thought you should get right away."

"What's the message?"

"About 8:30 some man called up, wanting you. When I told him this was your answering service, he said to be sure and give you the message. He said it was from the boys at Skip's." She paused. " 'You're dead.' "

"That was the message?"

"That was it. Just those two words: 'You're dead.' I even had him repeat it to make sure I got it right. He said you'd under-stand."

"I understand," I said. "Thanks."

"I'm sorry if I disturbed you, but I thought you'd want to know about it."

"Yes, thanks," I said and hung up.

I found that I could now unbutton my pants without swaying at all. I finished undressing and got into bed and turned out the lights. It was a long time before I went to sleep.

CHAPTER FIFTEEN

I opened my eyes into a gray, early-morning light and squinted at the alarm clock. I had beaten the hack by 20 minutes.

I struggled up and sat on the edge of the bed for a few minutes, tasting the cotton swabs that filled my mouth and trying to ride out the waves of pain that crashed intermittently against the inside of my head.

I went into the bathroom and took three aspirins, then came back out and put on some coffee. I stood over it, while it dripped through the grinds, then filled a thermos mug and sat down at the breakfast table. After one cup I felt like Lon Chaney after his first spoonful of tana leaves—coming alive, but not quite there. I refilled the cup and took it into the bathroom.

A hot-cold shower finished the job the coffee had started. I was just starting to shave when the phone rang.

It was Sergeant Williams. He apologized for calling so early but said he wanted to make sure he caught me. He wanted to know if he could come over this morning and take a statement from me. I told him that it wouldn't be necessary, that I would be coming downtown anyway and that I could stop at Parker Center on my way. We set a time at ten and said good-bye.

I finished shaving and got dressed and left the apartment. I pulled into a coffee shop on the way in, to get some breakfast. I bought a morning edition of the *Chronicle* from the stand outside and went inside and took a booth by the window.

I ordered scrambled eggs and toast and coffee from the waitress and went through the paper, looking for something on the Farnsworth killing. I found it on page four, headlined: "Possible Cult Links in Deprogrammer Slaying."

The article didn't tell me much I didn't already know. It said that Farnsworth had been found murdered in his apartment yesterday by the manager of the building and a "friend of the victim." The coroner estimated that he had been dead at least three days, although an autopsy would be performed today to formally determine the time and cause of death. Because of the bloody message the killer had left on the walls, police spokesmen said that it was "possible" that the murder had been the work of a "religious nut or group of nuts" seeking revenge for Farnsworth's deprogramming activities. It ended with a statement by Farnsworth's former wife, from whom he had been divorced for about a year, saying that Farnsworth used to receive at least "two or three death threats a month" from fanatical religious groups and that she thought the murder was perpetrated by "one of those groups."

I mulled over the article while I ate breakfast. By the time I finished, it was almost 9:30. I paid my check and left.

The four uniformed cops who stood inside the big glass front doors of Parker Center watched me intently as I walked in, maybe because I looked like the Mad Bomber type. I told the cop behind the reception desk that I had an appointment with Sergeant Williams of Robbery-Homicide, and he called upstairs to verify it. After checking out my driver's license, he issued me a plastic visitor's pass and told me to take the elevator up.

Robbery-Homicide was on the third floor. The cop on the front desk there pointed me to the back of the long room when I asked for Sergeant Williams. Williams' "desk," in front of a wall of filing cabinets, was part of a 20-foot-long table, one of three such tables in the room. He was sitting in a chair on one side of it, holding the phone up to his ear with one hand and a Styrofoam cup full of black coffee in the other. He was in his shirtsleeves. The front of his shirt was wrinkled and marked with occasional coffee stains, but his eyes didn't seem to be so badly out of alignment today.

"Glad you could make it," he said, putting down the phone and standing up. "It saved me a trip. Let's go down the hall."

He left his coffee on the table, and I followed him down the hall into a small interview room. We sat down at one of the tables, in front of a cassette tape machine. He inserted a cartridge and got a test level. He held the microphone while I went through my story again. When I got to the end, he stopped the recorder and stared at me. "Before you put your name to this, you want to think, just to make sure you haven't forgotten anything?"

"Like what?"

"Oh, I don't know," he said, shrugging. "You kind of forgot to tell me about Susan Gurney's arrest record and about her past association with the Satan's Warriors."

We watched each other for a few seconds in silence, then I said: "I didn't forget to tell you about her arrest."

He lifted a curious eyebrow. "No?"

"No. I didn't tell you on purpose."

"Yeah? Why is that?"

"Because I wouldn't get many jobs if I started shooting my mouth off about my clients' personal lives to the first cop who came along talking tough. Besides, I didn't think it had anything to do with this case—"

"You never know what's relevant in a murder case," he snapped.

"True enough," I relented. "But it's your job to determine what's relevant and what isn't, not mine. You wouldn't expect me to make those kinds of judgments when my client's interests are at stake."

"It seems you have a history of withholding information in murder cases, Asch. I kept thinking you looked familiar to me yesterday. After I left Farnsworth's apartment I did some checking on you. It seems you spent six months in the slammer for withholding information in a case a couple of years back while you were working for the *Chronicle*."

"Number one," I said, "there wasn't any *case*. The story I did was on a trial. The case had already been put together in a nice, neat little package. Number two, I wasn't thrown in jail for withholding information about any murder. The story was about a point of judicial procedure, and I was cited for contempt by a fascist prick of a judge who wanted me to name my sources for it. No charges were ever filed against me, and I never got a trial. Just six months in the slammer."

"And that's why you're peeping through keyholes now instead of working as the star reporter for the *Chronicle*."

"That's it," I said, trying to control my anger. He was trying to bait me, and I wanted to know why.

"What have you found out about the Gurney girl?"

"Since yesterday? Nothing."

"Nothing?"

"You ever try to find one girl in a city of four million people, sergeant? It's easy. Just one, two, three, a snap of the fingers, and she appears in a puff of smoke, just like a jinni from a bottle."

He grunted and fixed me with a cold stare.

"Look, sergeant, this isn't accomplishing anything for either of us. Why don't we stop acting like a couple of idiots and talk to one another like human beings?"

He drummed his fingers on the top of the table, then reached into his shirt pocket and pulled out a pack of Marlboros. He gave a sharp flick of the wrist and two cigarettes popped up. He took one and offered me the other. When I declined, he put the pack back into his pocket and lit the one in his mouth. "I'm listening," he said, exhaling a cloud of smoke.

I recited the story Haynes had told me about Farnsworth coming to him for money a few days before he was killed, knowing he would be getting it from Haynes anyway, if he had not gotten it already, hoping to break the ice. He listened attentively. When I finished, he said: "Why didn't you tell me all this yesterday?"

"Because I didn't know it then. I only learned about it later that afternoon."

"How?"

"Haynes told me."

He nodded mechanically and took another drag off his cigarette. "I talked to Haynes last night. He tells about the same story you do. It all fits. We found Farnsworth's checkbook. Haynes paid him the five hundred all right. The only question now is whether Farnsworth was really looking for his stepdaughter at the time he was knocked off or whether he was just bullshitting Haynes to see if he could shake a little more money off the money tree."

"I know the guy was edgy, but you think he was that edgy?"

He smiled. "A person will do just about anything when he's desperate, and Farnsworth was desperate. He had $487.50 in the bank at the time he was killed, which means that he'd already dipped into the five hundred Haynes had given him. He owed his wife three months' back alimony and child support and about every lawyer in town."

"The deprogramming business must not have been all that it was cracked up to be."

"It wasn't the business that was bad. It was what went with it. Everybody in the world was suing the shit out of the guy. Everything he was taking in was going right out to take care of his legal costs. Hell, at least four kids he had snatched and failed to deprogram had suits for kidnaping and assault pending against him, and a couple of religious communes were being backed up by the ACLU in suits they'd brought against Farnsworth, claiming he was violating their followers' First Amendment freedoms."

"If things were that bad, why did he stick with it?"

"From what his ex-wife told me, he thought he could make it pay off if he could only squeak through the next year. He was winning the cases, and he was convinced a big court decision was coming up that would open things up for him."

"So what's the story with Susan Gurney? Why are you so interested in her?"

"She's only one of the people I'm interested in. I'm interested in anybody Farnsworth had contact with in the last six months."

His eyes scanned the tabletop like a chameleon looking for flies. They converged on an ashtray at the end of the table. He pulled it over to him with a boardinghouse reach and ground his half-smoked cigarette in it.

"Why? From what I read in the paper this morning, you guys seem pretty sure that Farnsworth was snuffed by a religious fanatic with an Avenging Angel complex."

His face darkened unhappily. "I read the article. The police spokesman quoted in it wasn't me. I wasn't even consulted." He paused and said: "It's a funny thing. Ten years ago, when I first became a detective, if I had mentioned 'cult murder' to anybody, they would have laughed me off the force. Now, hell, since the department got caught with its pants down on the Manson thing, everybody's all jumpy we're going to get caught again, so they go off and release these bullshit stories."

"Then you don't think it was a cult killing?"

"I didn't say that. In those days, people still killed for love or money. Now, they kill for any fucking reason no matter how screwy."

"So what's your theory about the murder?"

106

"I don't have one."

I didn't believe him, but I didn't think he would have appreciated me telling him that. "Have you talked to Sievers yet?"

"No. I've been making some inquiries, though. Sheriff's Intelligence in Ventura County has quite a fat file on Sievers."

"And?"

He shrugged. "The general consensus is that the guy isn't just a rip-off artist. They seem to think he's a genuine, dyed-in-the-wool fanatic."

"I might go along with that," I said. "But fanatic or not, Sievers isn't stupid. If he wanted Farnsworth out of the way, I doubt he would have had it done like that, with everything but a roadmap spread out by the body, showing how to get out to the Word of God."

"Like I said, fanatics do funny things. Anyway, you didn't hear me say I thought Sievers had anything to do with anything, did you? There are a few coincidences that tie him in with Farnsworth, but those coincidences might just be that; they don't have to mean anything at all. For all I know, some fucking nut, or even somebody he knew, who hated him enough to kill him and wanted to make it look like the work of a nut, could have blown him away."

"What do you mean, 'blown him away?' You mean he was shot?"

"That's right. The autopsy report came in this morning. Farnsworth was killed by three .38 slugs in the chest. He took them at pretty close range, too. One went right through the aorta; the other two passed through the left lung."

"What about the knife?"

"That was stuck in him later. For effect, apparently. We've traced it down: it came from his own kitchen drawer."

"Have they fixed a time of death yet?"

"Between forty-eight and sixty-two hours before we found him."

"That's quite a bit of leeway."

"When a stiff is that far gone, it's hard to pin down."

"Do you have any theories as to why the killer would turn up the heat like that?"

"Not unless it was to throw the coroner off. Why are you so interested in the time of death, anyway?"

"I'm not, particularly. Just curiosity."

He watched me intently, trying to read my thoughts, but I put my most impassive face forward and he soon gave up. "You still haven't told me why you're so interested in Susan Gurney," I said.

He leaned back in his chair and hooked his thumbs underneath his belt. "Like I said, there are a few coincidences I'd like to get cleared up."

"Like what?"

"Oh, that Farnsworth was supposed to have been looking for her at the time he was killed. And that he was murdered a very short time after he'd ripped her off from the Word of God. And that either on the day of the murder or the day before—we're not sure which because of the autopsy reports—Farnsworth made a phone call to Eric Gurney at his office."

That one took me by surprise. "What about, do you know?"

"I know what Eric Gurney *says* it was about. He says Farnsworth called him up and said he had something very important to discuss with him. He wouldn't say what, just that it had something to do with the girl. An appointment was set up for the next day, but Farnsworth never showed."

"Are you implying that Susan Gurney's disappearance and the murder are linked up in some way?"

He sighed heavily. "Nope. I wouldn't go that far. Not yet, anyway. But I'm going to want to talk to the girl when and if she shows up. And I'm going to want to be kept informed of anything you turn up that might be involved in this case. I don't care how trivial you might think it is. And I'm not going to want to have to track you down and twist your arm to get it. You get my drift?"

"Consider it gotten, sergeant."

He studied my face, then picked up the microphone from the table and handed it to me. "Here. Put your name to this and you can get the hell out of here."

I smiled and took it out of his hand.

CHAPTER SIXTEEN

Since I was downtown anyway, I decided to see what kind of mail had collected on my office floor.

The sidewalks of Seventh Street were alive with people jostling from work to lunch and back, the dreary, cheerless gray of the buildings reflected in their faces. The elevator doors stood open as I entered the lobby. I stepped through them and pushed the button for the fourth floor. Mr. Rothblatt, a furrier, was locking the door of his shop as I stepped out into the dim hallway. He straightened up and smiled as I walked past him and said hello, and then shuffled away toward the elevator.

I unlocked my door and bent down to pick up the four days of mail that had accumulated underneath the mail slot. Four letters. One letter a day. If this kept up, I was going to have to hire a secretary just to handle my correspondence.

The air trapped in the office was hot and still. I dropped the mail on the desk and opened the window. Cool air rushed in, carrying with it the sounds of downtown traffic and wisps of cold steam from the clothes presses of Silverline Slacks, Incorporated, on the floor below.

I took off my coat and sat down and started going through the mail. One telephone bill for $35.41, two flyers from wholesale fabric dealers in the building, announcing clearance sales on bolts of quality cotton, and a form letter from Father O'Connor's Boys Farm, pleading for a donation so that God's work rehabilitating the world's lost souls could continue. I filed the phone bill under "Payables" and the rest in the waste basket, then picked up the phone and called my answering service.

I had had two calls in the morning—one from an Eric Gurney who wanted me to call him at his office at my convenience, and one from somebody named Gypsy. He hadn't left a number but said he would call back later.

I called Gurney. He said he had something to discuss with me and asked if I could come by his office that afternoon around four. When I asked him what it was about, all he would say was that it concerned Susan and that it was important. I told him I would be there and said good-bye.

I made coffee on my hot plate and settled down to wait for Gypsy. At a quarter to two the silence was sliced by the ringing of the phone. I picked it up. "Asch Investigations."

"Yeah, man," the raspy voice said. "This is Gypsy. I hear you been looking for me."

"Really? Where did you hear that?"

"From some friends of mine. What the fuck do you want?"

"First of all, I want to make sure you're really Gypsy."

"Whaddya mean?"

"Just what I said. I'm a very skeptical person. What's your middle name?"

There was a pause. "Lee."

"Where were you born?"

"What the fuck is this? Twenty questions?"

"Something like that. Where were you born?"

"Indiana, man. Valparaiso, Indiana."

"Okay," I said. "I'm looking for Susan Gurney."

"I don't know the chick."

"That's funny. I've got a copy of a letter right here that you wrote from the county jail saying that you do know the chick and very well at that. As a matter of fact, it says that as soon as you get out of jail, you're going to pick her up and put her on the back of your chopper and ride off into the sunset."

"Who're you working for, man?"

"Susan's parents."

"Where'd you get that letter?"

"From the desk in Susan's bedroom. She left it there when she ran away from home last week. You know, I'd be willing to bet that your probation officer would be very disappointed to hear that you were hanging around with Gurney again. Especially after all the trouble you two got into before."

"Fucker," he snarled, "if you're not careful, they could be picking your ass up in paper bags."

I sighed. "Where do you get your dialogue, Hunter? Abbey Rents? You want to talk or not?"

"We've got nothing to talk about, man."

"Sure we do. Susan Gurney. I told you."

"I ain't seen the chick since before I went into County, man. And that letter don't prove I have."

"The girl was with you at your apartment a few days ago, Hunter, so let's cut out all the bullshit and get down to basics."

"Yeah? Who says so?"

"A couple of people who identified her from her picture," I said. "And they've already put it in writing."

There was another pause, this time a long one, and then he said: "There's a bar in Culver City, on Venice Boulevard, called The Castle. I'll be there at seven o'clock. And bring that letter, man."

Before I had a chance to say anything, the line went dead. I hung up the phone and thought about the conversation and the designated meeting tonight with a twinge of anxiety. I didn't like the setup, especially after the message his buddies had left with my answering service the night before. Had Hunter not hung up so fast, I would have insisted on a neutral spot for the meeting, but that was a moot point now. Of course, I could always just not show up and wait for him to call back, but then he might never call back at all.

"Shit," I said out loud and stood up.

It was a few minutes after four when I stepped off the elevator onto the twelfth floor of the Cal Fed Building. Gurney's secretary told me to go right in.

The office was warm. Gurney was sitting at his desk in his shirt-sleeves. He looked less coldly self-assured than the last time I had seen him, and there seemed to be a hesitancy in his movements, in the way he smiled and stood up and offered his hand. I could feel the tenseness in his arm when I took the hand.

"Thanks for coming up, Asch," he said. "Sit down."

I sat in one of the chairs, and he resumed his place behind the desk, folding his hands neatly on its top. "The reason I asked you to come up is that I, uh, need some information. And some advice."

He paused and his eyes dropped down to his folded hands on the desk.

"You said it was about Susan—"

He looked up and nodded stiffly. "Yes, it is. Last night, two police detectives came by the house, wanting to know if I had seen or heard from Susan. I told them I hadn't. Then they started grilling me about a phone conversation I'd had with Farnsworth a few days ago. They said they'd pulled my number from his phone bill. I told them he'd called up at the office and said he had some information about Susan that I would be interested in and that I agreed to meet him for lunch the next day, but he never showed up. After I told that to the police, they told me that Farnsworth had been murdered. It really gave me a good jolt. I mean, I didn't have any use for the man, but to go like that, it's, it's horrible—"

He shook his head, and his face screwed up as if he were thinking what it would be like to have a carving knife inserted in his own body.

"You have no idea what Farnsworth wanted to talk to you about?"

"No. He didn't say what it was other than it involved Susan. Then when the police asked me about it, I naturally thought that they were looking for Susan because they thought she might have had something to do with the murder. I kept asking them, but the detective in charge—Williams or Williamson or something—kept saying that it was purely routine, that they just wanted to talk to her to ask her a few questions. I believed him, but then something came up this morning which made me think I was right in the first place. I knew it would be useless to try to get anything out of Cynthia, so I phoned you."

"What came up?"

"I'll get to that in a minute," he said. "First, I want to know whether Susan is mixed up in this Farnsworth thing."

"I don't know, Mr. Gurney," I said. "All I can tell you is that I talked to Williams this morning and he gave me exactly the same story he gave you, that they were just looking for her as part of a routine homicide investigation."

"Well, I don't know. I had the distinct impression when I talked to him that he was holding something back. I've been in the insurance business for twenty years. You get to know about people, whether they're holding something back. I could see it in Williams' face; he thought that if I knew Susan was in trouble, I wouldn't tell him where she was."

"Would you?"

112

"Of course I would," he said without hesitation. "There's no running away from something like this." He fixed me with a gray stare. "But before I told them, I'd make goddamn sure she had a good lawyer on hand."

I nodded. "I don't mean for you to take this wrong, Mr. Gurney, but why exactly did you call me?"

"Because I thought you'd be likely to know what's going on." He paused and then said: "I also felt I could trust you to tell me the truth."

I wondered from what fountain his newfound trust had sprung. Maybe from desperation. Maybe he felt he had to trust somebody, so he had covered his eyes, pointed a finger, and come up with me. I felt a sudden twinge of shame at my own hard-bitten cynicism. You're a trustworthy son of a bitch, Asch, I thought, why shouldn't somebody trust you? I was about to live up to my trustworthy, truthful image and tell him about Haynes having hired Farnsworth to look for Susan, but then checked myself, getting mental flashes of angry recriminations flying back and forth between the two armed camps and a quick, sweet phone call from Cynthia Haynes informing me that my services would no longer be required.

"As far as I can see, Mr. Gurney, there's no reason to believe Susan is involved. It's only natural, considering the circumstances, that the cops would want to talk to her."

That didn't seem to allay his fears. "You say you talked to Williams this morning. Does he have any suspects in the case?"

"Not that he's telling me about. Not that he would tell me if he did."

"What about those people out at the commune? Aaron Sievers and that bunch? The papers say the police think Farnsworth might have been killed by one of the cults he was working against."

"As a former reporter, I can tell you that cult murders make good copy. Anytime you get a kinky sex or religious angle into a murder, people are going to eat it up. It adds a flavor of Gothic romance to a normally sordid and degrading act."

He shifted nervously in his chair. "But what about that writing in blood on the walls?"

"Anybody can write on walls," I said, shrugging.

113

"Then you don't think the Word of God had anything to do with Farnsworth's murder?"

"Are you asking me for my personal guess?"

"Yes."

"Then I'd have to say I don't think it's likely, although I wouldn't throw it out completely as a possibility."

He shifted again in his chair. He was leading up to something. I could feel it. "Look, why are you so interested in the Word of God?"

He stared at me and his face seemed to suddenly grow longer. "Because Susan is back there."

"How do you know?"

He opened his desk drawer and pulled out an envelope and handed it to me without looking at it. "I got this this morning in the mail."

I took the envelope out of his hands and looked at it. Gurney's name and home address were written across the front in a woman's slanting hand. It was postmarked Fillmore, but there was no return address. I opened the flap and removed a sheet of plain white typing paper.

Dear Dad,

I haven't written before this because I wasn't sure where you stood in my life. I've been doing some thinking about it and praying for guidance and I see now that you've had your own life to lead and couldn't be bothered with me. I understand that and forgive you your past sins against me. I'm just writing to tell you that I'm happy and safe in the arms of Jesus and everything is OK. Cynthia tried to tear me away but I'm back in His arms now, filled with the Holy Spirit. Don't send anybody to look for me please and don't *under any circumstances* tell Cynthia and Robert about this letter. They'd only try to spoil my chances for happiness. I know you may not understand everything I've written, but if you care about me, you'll let me work things out my own way. I'll come and see you soon and explain better.

Love, Susie

I finished the letter, then read it through again more slowly. The wording had a contrived, melodramatic sound to it that bothered me. It didn't jibe somehow with the mental picture I had built up of Susan Gurney. Not that the mental picture I had built up was necessarily accurate. "You say you got this this morning?"

"It came with the morning mail," he said, nodding stiffly. "I didn't know what to do about it. That's why I called you. I didn't want to do anything until I found out what the situation was with the . . . police."

"What *are* you going to do?"

He rubbed his upper lip with an index finger and said: "Go out to the Word of God tonight and demand to see Susan and try to talk her into coming out of there. She may not even be aware that Farnsworth is dead. They live a cloistered life out there. They aren't even allowed to read newspapers."

"And if she doesn't want to leave? What are you going to do then?"

The resolution he had summoned in his voice suddenly dissipated, and lines of uncertainty drew his mouth down at the corners into a dark frown. "I don't know. All I know is that I've got to try. If you're wrong and Sievers and his people did have something to do with the Farnsworth thing, then Susan is in with a bunch of fanatical murderers. She may be in danger—"

"I doubt she's in any physical danger," I said. "If she was, she wouldn't have been allowed to mail that letter. But I'd be interested to hear what Sievers has to say about this." I handed him back the letter and envelope, and he put them back in his desk drawer. "Can I call you in the morning?"

"Sure."

"What time?"

"It doesn't matter. I'm always up by seven. Do you have my home phone?"

"Yeah, I've got it," I said. "I should know more by tomorrow, too. I've been tracing your daughter's movements during the past week, and I should have most of what she has been doing pieced together by then. We can compare notes and go from there."

We both stood up and shook hands. "I take it I can trust you not to mention anything about this letter to Cynthia—"

"Don't worry," I said. "I'll talk to you tomorrow."

He looked relieved. "Thanks for coming by."

"No problem," I said and waved good-bye as I went out the door.

CHAPTER SEVENTEEN

The Castle shared a block on Venice Boulevard with some moderately priced apartment buildings, a health food store, and two karate schools, which was probably a testimonial to the bar's clientele. It was a white building, the top of which was crenellated to resemble the battlements of a castle, with a wood façade covering its lower half. A series of lighted signs festooned the battlements, advertising the delights awaiting within: BEER, DANCING, POOL, DARTS. A white arrow composed of dozens of tiny light bulbs, half of which were burned out, flashed on and off, pointing at the front door. Another sign, this one unlighted and crudely hand-painted on plywood, was nailed to the façade and read: GIRLS GIRLS GIRLS.

I cruised by the place slowly, checking it out, then circled the block and cruised by again.

There were a couple of pickup trucks and a lowered Chevy parked in the small lot beside the building. No bikes. I swung around and parked across the street and watched the bar from there. I looked at my watch. 6:50.

At five after seven, a chopped Harley roared up the street and pulled into The Castle's parking lot. The lone rider fit Hunter's description. He was wearing a sleeveless jacket with the Warriors' colors on the back and a long-sleeved Pendleton shirt, presumably for warmth. He parked the bike and put down the kickstand, then went inside.

I waited another five minutes, then got out of the car and crossed the street.

The interior of the bar had all the quaint charm of a sheep dip. It had a high, plaster ceiling, a dirty linoleum tile floor, and bare, oak-paneled walls. The only artistic decoration in the place was the Coors sign with the lighted waterfall tumbling down its face. Two pool tables, lighted by overhead fluorescents suspended from the ceiling, stood next to the bar. Around them several men were standing, chalking up their pool cues and sizing up their shots. A few others tossed darts at a board on the wall. But most of the clientele were sitting at the cocktail tables that occupied the center of the barn-like room, watching a nude girl work out on the tiny stage.

She was dark-haired and overweight. Her huge breasts rolled and swayed listlessly as she pumped her hips in time to the Rolling Stones number blaring from the jukebox. The number ended, and one or two of the audience applauded weakly. She stood with a glazed, faraway look in her eyes, her jaws working belligerently on a wad of chewing gum, waiting for the next record to come on. It did, and her hips started their piston-like movements again. I went to the bar.

About halfway through the smoke and noise of the room, I spotted Hunter at the bar. He was standing with his back to me, his fingers coiled around the glass handle of a beer mug. I came up next to him at the bar and ordered a beer. He watched me as the bartender brought the beer and I put down a bill. I waited until the bartender had returned with my change before I said anything to him.

"Gypsy?"

"I'm Gypsy," he said. "You Asch?"

I nodded and took a better look at him. His face was thin and ferret-like, framed by a head of straight brown hair that was held out of his eyes by a beaded Indian headband. He had a full mustache that curled down over the edges of his mouth; about a two-day stubble showed on the rest of his face. His large, green eyes were set far apart on his head, which, combined with his small, turned-down mouth, gave him all the lovability of a hammerhead shark.

"You want to take a table?" I suggested.

He picked up his mug without answering and walked away. I followed him over to a tiny cocktail table away from the jukebox, and we sat down.

"So what's your story, man?" he asked. "Why are you trying to hassle me?"

"I'm not trying to hassle you," I said loudly, trying to be heard over the music. "I'm trying to save you from being hassled—remember?"

He took a swig from his mug. When he put it down, there was a residue of white foam on his mustache, giving him the appearance of a rabid dog. He wiped the foam off with the sleeve of his shirt and said: "I guess you're out of luck, man, cause I don't know where Sue is."

"We're not going to have to go through all that again, are we? I told you she was seen with you by reliable witnesses."

He leaned across the table and sneered. "Fuck them witnesses, man. Just because the chick was with me a couple of days ago, that don't mean she's with me now, does it?"

"Okay," I said. "If she's not with you, where is she?"

He threw his hands up in a contemptuous shrug. "She could be anywhere, man. She split two days ago. She didn't leave no forwarding address."

"Split from where?"

"From the pad we were staying at."

"Where is that?"

He glowered at me and said: "At a friend's."

"What friend?"

"That's none of your fucking business, man."

"Okay," I said. "How did she leave? Was she walking?"

He shook his head. "I wasn't there, man. I was out when she split. She could have jammed with some other dude for all I know."

"You don't sound as if you care that she left," I said.

He leaned over toward me again and said: "Look, I'm not going to chase no cunt around like some asshole, man. If the chick wants to come back, she knows where to find me."

"What happened that made her leave? You two have an argument?"

He looked down at his beer and then picked it up and took another drink from it. "We had a little beef, yeah. She said some things I didn't like, so I hit her. I guess that pissed her off, because I took off on my bike, just to get out of there, you know, man, and when I got back, she'd split."

"What did she say that you didn't like?"

His eyes narrowed. "That's none of your fucking business, either."

I smiled. It was an effort. "And you've got no idea where she might have gone?"

"That's what I said, man. You hard of hearing or something?"

"As a matter of fact, I am. Left ear."

He leaned toward my right and said loudly: "Well, I'm talking to your right ear now, fucker. I got no idea where she's gone. Period. End of message. You want to find her, go check with her Jesus freak buddies, man. They might know where she is."

"You mean the people at the Word of God?"

He nodded and chugged some beer.

"Why do you think they might know?"

He leaned back and stroked his mustache thoughtfully. "Because Sue was still zapped out on all that Jesus shit. That was one reason we got into a hassle that night. I tried to tell her it was a bum trip, that Sievers was just running a big rip-off, but she couldn't dig it, man. She just couldn't shake her head loose from all that Bible shit."

"So you think she went back to the Word?"

"I don't think nothing, man," he said.

I believed that.

The number on the jukebox ended, and the dancer stopped jiggling her tits and turned her back on the audience. She got into a bra and black bikini panties that were draped over a chair at the back of the stage, then stepped off the stage. She walked over to the bar and said something to the bartender, who laughed, then she picked up a cocktail tray and began cruising the room, taking drink orders. Her face was as expressionless as death; looking at it depressed me. I turned back to Hunter.

"Susan was living at the Word when you got out of jail, right?"

"Yeah, that's right," he said. He killed off the rest of the beer in the mug, then put the glass back down on the table and belched.

"How did you happen to find out where she was?"

He gave me a bored look and said: "A buddy of mine saw her on Hollywood Boulevard handing out pamphlets, and he told me about it. I cruised a couple of nights until I found her. No great mystery, man."

"Sievers says you visited her at the commune."

"So?"

"He also says you slipped her some grass on one of those visits."

"Yeah? Well, that's his story."

"What's yours?"

"I have a beer every once in a while, man, but that's all. I wouldn't mess with dope or anything that was bad for me like that."

He showed me some nicotine-stained teeth. I said: "Sievers told me you came back up to the commune looking for Susan after she'd been taken away. He said you had some of your buddies with you and threatened to take the place apart. That true?"

He shrugged. "I thought he was trying to shit me, and I didn't like the idea. I took about twenty of the brothers and we went on a casual little run up there to see what was happening, you know? There wasn't no trouble."

"You thinking of taking another run up there in the near future?"

"What for? If Sue's up there now, she's there under her own power, man. She knows how to get back."

He looked over my shoulder, toward the door, and a small smile crossed his lips. I turned to see what he was looking at. It turned out to be a bearded giant wearing a Warriors jacket. He must have been six-six or seven and weighed close to three hundred. He stood taking up the whole doorway, eyeing the room. When his eyes fell on Hunter, he nodded slightly and walked over to the bar. When I turned back around, Hunter was getting up.

"I'm tired of answering your questions, man," he said. "Go ask'em to somebody else."

Something was in the air, and I didn't like it. "One more question before you go, Hunter. You own a .38?"

He squinted down at me. "Ain't you heard, man? I'm on probation. I'm not allowed to own guns. Why, what's all this shit about a .38?"

"Nothing. I was just wondering. Larry Farnsworth was murdered with a .38, that's all."

"I never heard of no Larry Farnsworth."

"Just like you'd never heard of Susan Gurney?" I said. "Larry Farnsworth was the deprogrammer who kidnaped Susan from the Word of God. Don't tell me she never mentioned him."

"Sure, she mentioned him. But I didn't even remember the dude's name, man. What's he got to do with me?"

"That's what I was asking you," I said as casually as possible. "Farnsworth was looking for Susan at the time he was murdered. I just thought that you might have heard about it, and being the possessively jealous type, you might have gone over to his apartment and put a couple of slugs in him to keep him from taking her away from you."

His face darkened like a gathering storm, and he said through clenched teeth: "You're fucking crazy, man. You're trying to pin some kind of a bullshit rap on me, and I'm not going for it." He stabbed a finger at me violently. "Remember what I'm telling you, man, and you remember good. If I get hassled by my P.O. or the pigs about Sue or this Farnsworth bullshit you just laid on me, you'd better go out and buy yourself a funeral plot somewhere, because it's going to be your *ass*."

"You know, Gypsy, for somebody who's trying to convince me he's a law-abiding, peaceable man who wouldn't do physical harm to anyone, you're doing a piss-ass poor job."

"You just remember, punk," he snarled and walked over to the bar to join his friend.

He ordered a beer and said something inaudible to the giant who turned and began pinning me out. I knew what his game was, and I didn't want any part of it, so I looked quickly away and stood up to go. I made my way through the stale sweat and smoke of the room to the door.

It took me one step outside for the realization to sink in that I had been had.

The parking lot was a sea of chrome—chromed handlebars and wire wheels, chromed sprockets and chains, chromed sissy bars and exhaust pipes. Ten bikes stood in a neat line, shining chrome, their radically raked front wheels all turned at neat right angles, their Warrior riders fanned out across the lot in front of them. The one I had taken for a ride on the hood of my car was standing in the center of the pack, grinning. The side of his face was a mass of ugly scabs, probably from where he had hit the pavement.

"Hi there, fuckface," he said. "Remember me?"

The others were smiling. Now I knew why Hunter and Mighty Joe Young inside had been smiling. They were all happy. They were going to kick some ass tonight.

I turned to go back into the bar, but the bodies of Hunter and the bearded giant had swallowed up the doorway. I turned toward the street, but four of the others moved to block my way.

I tried to think of something fast, but all I could come up with was to get back inside. I sidestepped the giant and tried for the door, but Hunter had anticipated my move and stepped in my way.

He was fast, I had to hand it to him. So fast I didn't even see his shoulder drop before the blow ripped into my gut with the force of a 20-pound sledge. I doubled over and gasped for air. A pair of hands grabbed me by the shoulders, and I was suddenly being propelled backward. I lost my footing and stumbled and went down hard.

I struggled to my feet, gasping for air, but by that time it was too late. The stomping circle had already been formed. My mind raced, but all I could think of was stall, stall, on the slim hope that somebody would come through the front door of the bar and see what was happening and go call the cops.

"You're just buying yourself a lot of trouble, Hunter," I managed between clenched teeth.

"I'm not buying myself nothing, motherfucker," he snarled. "You already bought it all by coming here. You don't just fuck with the Warriors and walk away in one piece. Not only did you try to hassle me, but we owe you for what you did to Crazy Marvin here."

"All you're going to get out of this is an assault rap," I said in a rather shaky voice.

He laughed, whether at my voice or what I was saying, I didn't know.

One of the others stepped forward and brought a tire iron from behind his back. I felt a spurt of adrenalin surge through my body as he came toward me. I kept my eyes glued on the weapon. He made a lunge forward, thrusting the iron at me menacingly, and I grabbed onto the end of it. He jerked the tool out of my hand then and straightened up and stepped back, smiling.

"That's got your prints on it now," Hunter said. "A clear case of self-defense, man. You pulled a tire iron on Marvin here, and he took it away from you."

The music from the jukebox inside grew suddenly loud as the door opened and a short, fat man came walking out. He froze when he saw what was happening.

"Call the cops," I told him.

The bearded giant glared down at the man and said: "This is a private affair. Get the fuck out of here."

The man scurried back inside.

"Let's get this fucking show on the road," the one called Crazy Marvin said, impatiently, moving forward.

He aimed a boot at my crotch, but I hopped back and he missed. Then he put his head down and came at me swinging. His shots were wild and sloppy, and I took my head out of the way of a long, looping right and came down with a short, chopping right of my own that landed solidly on the left side of his chin. The blow didn't travel any more than a foot, but it was well-timed and whatever of his weight had not sailed by me with that right hand of his met my fist head on. He staggered back and fell, but I didn't have time to feel good about it because something hit me hard on the back of the head and I lurched forward, only to meet a fist with my eye. I felt the blood warm and wet run down my face from the cut that had opened above my eye. Then another fist caught me on the side of the head and another one in the neck and two more on the cheekbone and I reeled sideways. I swung out blindly, but all I drew was air. Then a blow grazed my shoulder and another one off the side of my head. I suddenly felt as if I were floating, but I knew I wasn't floating; I was falling.

I hit the pavement, and they were yelling and grunting above me and the boots started ripping into my body. All I could do was cover my head with my hands to try to protect my head. Then there was a shooting pain in my left elbow and my arm went dead and another boot ripped into my kidneys and I knew this was going to be it.

Then I heard somebody yelling above their yelling: "Okay, okay, break it up, goddamn it. That's enough. That's enough!"

The boots stopped tearing into me, and the voice said: "You want to kill the son of a bitch?"

"The asshole shithead deserves it, Eddie," another voice said. "He tried to pull a tire iron on Crazy Marvin. Show him the tire iron, Little John. See? We had to teach him a lesson."

"Not on my fucking property, you don't. The cops are just waiting for an excuse to close me up, goddamn it. You want them to close me up? One more of these numbers, and I swear to God, I'll declare this place off limits to you guys."

"Okay, okay. Drag the fucker off Eddie's property, fellas. We'll finish the job in the street."

"You want to kill the son of a bitch?" Eddie's voice asked. "He's had enough. Look at him. Look, you guys, come inside and I'll buy you a beer."

Their voices weaved together in a confused tangle, some going for Eddie's idea, some protesting that they would rather stay and finish the job they had started. The issue was decided by the sound of a siren, far off, slicing the night with its shrill cry.

"Great," Eddie said. "Now the fucking cops are coming."

"Did you call the pigs, Eddie?"

"What, are you crazy? You think I want to get closed down?"

"That little fat mother must have called them," one of the others said.

Then Eddie's voice: "I don't give a shit who called them. They're coming, and now my ass is in a ringer."

"Don't worry, Eddie," Hunter's voice said. "We'll explain it all to the pigs. Let's go inside and have a brew. Little John, bring in that tire iron to show the pigs when they get here."

Their voices went away from me, laughing and talking. Then the music from the bar poured over me and with their laughter grew muted again.

CHAPTER EIGHTEEN

The siren was close now, slicing the night with its shrill cry. I uncurled myself painfully from my fetal position and with a monumental effort struggled to my hands and knees and raised my head. I tried to focus my vision, but everything kept rolling up toward the night sky like a television picture with a broken vertical hold. I felt as if everything in my body had been broken twice.

The siren reached a piercing crescendo, and I got a glimpse of the flashing red lights and the sleek red and white body as the car screamed past the bar and continued on down Venice Boulevard. I gasped out a half-choked laugh. An ambulance. Now *that* was a good joke. It was too bad the others weren't out here so I could share it with them.

The laugh had shaken something loose in my chest and I sucked in air sharply and started to cough. I managed to get the cough controlled after a few seconds and spat out a mouthful of blood. I felt a spurt of fear when I saw the blood and ran my tongue across my teeth, but breathed easier when I felt nothing chipped. At least that. My teeth were one of the few prized possessions I could still call my own.

I stayed there on my hands and knees, waiting for the dizziness to abate enough so that I could stand without falling. The ambulance had granted me a reprieve, but I had no idea how long the reprieve would be. I knew I had to get the hell out of there and fast.

I made it to my feet. The legs underneath me were not mine, but they were holding. I started shakily toward the driveway. The broken stream of headlights coming down Venice Boulevard were blurry. I waited for a complete lull of darkness before braving the wilds of the street. I made the center divider all right and rested there before starting across the second lap of two lanes.

I found my car and after a lengthy search through my pockets for the keys, got in and pulled out into traffic. My head had partially cleared, but I still felt dizzy and nauseous. I crept along in the slow lane, fighting the wheel to keep the car from weaving over the dotted line. Then I saw the nine-story tower of Westside Community Hospital up ahead on the right and made for it like a homing pigeon.

I found the emergency entrance at the end of a narrow ambulance alley and parked my car crookedly in one of the spaces in the adjacent parking lot and wobbled back to the entrance.

A hefty, starch-faced nurse was sitting guard on the admittance desk when I came in. She looked me over woodenly and asked me if I was covered by Blue Cross or Blue Shield or any other health insurance plan. After we had gotten it straight that I was not and after she had satisfied herself that I understood that there was a minimum emergency room fee of $13.25, payable in advance, plus a minimum doctor's fee of $14, she asked me what had happened.

I was about to tell her but then thought better of it. She would immediately call the cops, and I didn't think Haynes would appreciate me handing them his stepdaughter's name again so soon. Besides, reporting the incident probably wouldn't get me anything except a couple of days in Parker Center, looking at lineups. It was my word against the word of ten of them, plus, in all probability, that of Eddie, the owner of The Castle, that I hadn't attacked anybody with a tire iron. Even if the cops believed me, the D.A. probably wouldn't even move to prosecute.

I told the nurse I had fallen off a motorcycle and she gave me a look which said that she either did not approve of me or approve of motorcycles or motorcycle-riding and handed me a form to fill out.

I took the form over to the wooden bench that lined the corridor wall and sat down next to two other men who were also filling out forms. One of them had one of his hands wrapped in a blood-soaked towel. The other, a sunken-chested old man whose frail frame shook with each loud, wheezing breath, did not look as if he were going to make it to the end of his form.

I handed in my form and paid my $27.50. Starch-face led me through the doors into the waiting room and told me to sit down.

126

The room was filled to capacity with fractured arms and bloody noses and cut fingers and a couple of cases of LSD heebie-jeebies.

I waited my turn and was finally led into the emergency room. A young doctor who had probably been up for two days and looked in worse shape than I did, took my blood pressure. After determining that I was not in shock, he put four stitches above my right eye and five in my scalp, took a look at my arm, and packed me off to X-ray.

The X-rays of my chest and arm came out negative, and the doctor said I could go home. But he warned me that I might have a slight concussion and told me to take it easy for a couple of days.

Starch-face sat at her desk, when I came out, her nose buried in a stack of papers. She didn't bother to look up as I passed. I pushed open the door and went out to the parking lot.

CHAPTER NINETEEN

I woke up the next morning knowing how Mussolini would have felt if he had lived, the poor dumb buffoon. My head felt as if it had been blown apart by an M–14, and my elbow was a swollen, throbbing mass of heat and pain. Struggling up, I went into the bathroom to survey the damage and found little consolation in the fact that the puffy, discolored face that floated above the sink looked worse than I felt. I quickly gave up the idea of trying to shave, took three of the Darvons the doctor had given me and went out to the kitchen for coffee.

As I sat at the breakfast table, I kept running over the past night in my mind, trying to pick out inconsistencies in Hunter's story. I couldn't find any, but I also couldn't shake the feeling that he had been lying. Maybe it was because I wanted to believe he was lying so that I would have an excuse to go after him to wreak my vengeance on him for what he had done to me, but I doubted it. I was pissed about it. Nobody likes having his face kicked in, especially by a bunch of jackbooted neo-Nazi cretins, but deep down I knew I wasn't at all eager to tackle the Satan's Warriors again so soon. Not when I could beat the shit out of ten of the bastards in my dreams without absorbing one painful, rib-crunching kick. One thing was certain: the next time I went looking for Hunter and his animal friends, I was going to be better prepared—like with a flamethrower and a bazooka.

I suddenly remembered that I was supposed to call Eric Gurney to find out how he made out with Sievers. I looked up his number in my book and dialed it. His wife answered and said just a minute when I asked for him. He picked it up after a lull of a few dozen seconds. "Hello?"

"Mr. Gurney, this is Asch. Did you talk to Sievers last night?"

"I talked to him," he said. "He flatly denied that Susan was there. He said he hasn't seen her since she was taken out of there by Farnsworth."

"Did you show him the letter?"

"Sure, I showed it to him. He just shrugged and said he didn't know anything about it. I even told him that if he didn't let me talk to her, I was going to turn the letter over to the police and let them tear the place apart looking for her, but that didn't have any effect on him either. He just shrugged and started spouting off some Bible shit to me until I finally gave up trying to talk to him and went home. I don't know what to think now." He paused and said: "What did you find out, anything?"

I told him briefly about Hunter, and he said: "Hell, that *proves* Sievers is lying."

"It would indicate that one of them is lying. I'm not sure which one."

"Why would this Hunter make up a story like that?"

"One reason—he's on probation. If his probation officer found out he's been sha—been hanging around with Susan again, it could mean a lot of trouble for him."

"You were going to say 'shacked up,' weren't you?"

"Yes."

"I see," he said thickly, then fell silent again. "I wish—oh, I don't know what the hell I wish."

Actually, Gurney probably had no real right to feel disappointed at his daughter choosing to live with a slimy bike bum like Hunter. He had stayed out of things for too long. But it was probably that knowledge that made it all the more painful for him to accept.

"What can we do?" he asked, his voice suddenly sounding tired.

"I'm going to go up to the Word of God and take a look around. Then I'm going to talk to Mr. Sievers. He's had a night to think about your threat to bring in the cops. Maybe he'll have changed his mind about things."

"And if he hasn't?"

"Then I look up Hunter again," I said.

"You'll keep me notified if something develops, won't you?"

"I'll call you tonight and tell you how things worked out. Bye."

I pulled on a pair of Levi's and a long-sleeved, wool shirt and went down to the car.

Early morning traffic on the San Diego Freeway was light,

heading out of town. I maintained a steady 60 through the north end of the valley. As I headed up the San Fernando Pass, I found myself driving into a wet, misty fog that moved down off the tops of the mountains and clung to their sides. At Newhall, a lighted 24-hour coffee shop sign peeped through the fog, and I swung down the off-ramp.

I bought a morning paper and scanned it over breakfast, searching for anything new on the Farnsworth murder but found nothing. By the time I had finished and paid my check, the sun was making a feeble showing through the overhead gloom.

The air had warmed up, and the last tendrils of mist were spiraling up from the surrounding orchards and burning off as I turned onto the road to the commune. The town looked different in the daytime—hardly ominous, just a series of dilapidated, dirty buildings leaning wearily against one another for support. I began the winding climb into the foothills.

One of the commune's station wagons was parked in the driveway of the house. Several white-shirted disciples were working on the grounds. One of them—a skinny, long-haired youth whose face was blazing with the fires of righteousness and acne—left his hedge and approached as I got out of the car.

"Can I help you, brother?"

"I'm here to see Brother Moses."

"Brother Moses isn't here right now. Can I help you?"

"It's kind of important that I talk to Brother Moses. He told me to come up."

He cocked his head to one side. "Well, he's not here. He went down to the beach to raise some souls from the dead."

"Pardon me?"

My confusion brought a renewed smile to his lips. "He went to baptize some new believers, brother. Through the rites of baptism, we are all raised from the dead by the glory of the Father and reborn in Christ."

"Oh. You have any idea when he might be back?"

He shrugged. "It should be a couple of hours. He just left a little while ago. Most everybody from the commune went."

"Would you happen to know what beach he went to?"

"Ventura State Beach, I think. That's where he usually does the baptisms."

I nodded. "Why didn't you go?"

He made a disappointed face. "Somebody had to stay around here and watch the place."

"How long have you been a disciple of the Word, brother?"

He smiled happily at my filial reference. "I found my way to the Lord almost four months ago. I was just wandering around the streets, lost and sick, and then I met the brothers and sisters from the Word."

"Maybe you know my niece," I said. "She found Jesus just about the same time you did. Sister Sarah?"

His smile turned into a frown and he said: "Sister Sarah? She hasn't been around here for weeks. She was taken out of here by her old man. Kidnaped." He paused and said: "Who did you say you were?"

"Her uncle. You're sure you haven't seen Sister Sarah around here recently?"

"No," he said in a sulky voice, misgivings growing on his face.

"Well, bless you, brother," I said, opening the car door. "You've been a great help."

He stood in the driveway, watching me back out. Only when I reached the street did he reluctantly walk back to his hedge and start back to work.

I hit fog again when I reached 101. I took the exit for Ventura State Beach and dipped under a bridge and drove along the beach.

I didn't have any trouble finding the baptism site. Two of the commune buses and one of the station wagons were in the parking spaces along the edge of the sand.

The air was cold and wet, and there was a nippy breeze blowing off the water. The beach was deserted except for a few peroxided surfers in sleeveless wetsuits who were straddling their boards beyond the breaker line, waiting for a good wave. I involuntarily sucked in a breath of air at the thought of stepping into that cold, gray surf and started my trek across the sand toward the crowd that was gathered by the water's edge next to the pier.

There must have been 60 or 70 people clustered along the shore. All but ten or eleven of them were members of the Word of God; the rest were just the curious who had wandered down to see what was going on. I came up behind two of these, an old couple who were bundled up in sweaters and mittens, and settled back to watch the show.

Sievers, Isaiah, and Abraham were about 20 yards out in the swell, standing waist-deep in their soaking white shirts, talking earnestly to three young converts, two boys and a girl. The three finished whatever they were saying. Their resurrectees nodded. Then Sievers and his lieutenants closed their eyes and started murmuring some incantation, putting their hands on the heads of the young proselytes and pushed them under the water.

Sievers' charge was a young, blond girl. When her head came up out of the water, a shout went up from the crowd, and everybody threw their arms around everybody else and embraced lovingly. The girl herself was crying for joy. She threw her arms around Sievers' neck, and he reassuringly draped an arm around her shoulder and led her gently toward the shore.

The members on the beach rushed forward and wrapped beach towels around the six wet figures. Then some of the other disciples started moving among the spectators, passing out Word of God literature. The old couple, seemingly bewildered by the whole episode, took one of the pamphlets when it was handed to them by a smiling, apple-cheeked girl, and moved off.

The girl came up to me. "Would you like to find the way to peace and happiness through our Lord Jesus Christ?"

"Sure."

"Then read this."

"Thanks," I said and took the pamphlet, walking away before she had a chance to get started.

I went over to the buses and waited, hoping to corner Sievers there. About five minutes later the group had dispensed their literature to all who were in the vicinity (except for the surfers, and nobody seemed willing to swim all the way out there just to give them a tract), and were heading back toward the buses. Sievers was at the head of the noisy pack, wiping his dripping beard and face with one end of an orange beach towel he wore like a shawl over his shoulders. I walked over to the station wagon, figuring that he had come in it.

"All right," he called to his flock, "everybody on the buses. Let's get moving." He watched them load and then came over to the station wagon. He stopped dead when he saw me.

132

"What are you doing here?" he asked sharply, striding over to where I was standing.

"It's obvious, isn't it? I'm here to talk to you."

"What about?"

"The same thing we talked about before. Susan Gurney."

"I already told you. I don't know where the girl is."

"I'm hardheaded. It takes awhile for things to sink in."

"I can see that," he said, pointing at my face. "It looks like somebody didn't like the questions you were asking. Or was it just the way you were asking them?"

"Maybe a little of both."

Isaiah came up and stood behind Sievers, his eyes seeming to tell me he was sorry that he hadn't been the one who had done the job on my face.

"I talked to Susan's boyfriend. He says she had a spiritual rebirth and left him to come back to your commune."

"Boyfriend? What boyfriend?"

"Her biker boyfriend—Gypsy."

Sievers raised an incredulous eyebrow. "That 8:44? And you'd believe him?"

I didn't have to know what book "8:44" came from to guess it was something nasty. "I wouldn't normally. But he's got a little corroborating evidence to back him up. That letter."

"That letter never mentioned the Word of God by name," he snapped.

"What are you saying, that the girl fell in with some other Jesus freaks?"

"I'm not saying anything. I don't know what the whole thing is about, and I don't care. The girl isn't with us. I've told you that and I've told her father that, and I don't intend to discuss it anymore."

He started to move around me. I said: "Look, Sievers, I just got through talking to the homicide detective in charge of the Farnsworth case. He wants to talk to the girl in the worst way. He wouldn't take it lightly if he thought you were hiding her from him for some reason. You're already high on his list of suspects. Now, I haven't told him about that letter yet—"

"So tell him," he said, throwing a hand deprecatingly in the air. "The cops have been on my back since the day I founded the Word of God. Their petty harassments don't bother me. As a matter of fact, I take courage from them. It just proves that the last days are upon us. The Bible says that the final days before the Judgment will be a time of great persecution for all those who live Godly in Jesus Christ. I'd feel left out if the Devil didn't single us out for his attention."

He sounded sincere, and I found myself half-believing him. But only half. Every time I found myself swinging toward belief, I remembered the kids on those buses who believed him, too, and I checked myself.

"Now listen, Asch, just so we don't have any more misunderstandings," he said, jabbing a finger at me. "I don't expect to see you around the Word of God or any of my members again. If I do, I'll consider you a trespasser and have you thrown off my property by force, if necessary. You got all that?"

"Loud and clear."

"Good," he said, and turned to Isaiah. "Let's go."

They went around me to the doors of the wagon, Isaiah purposely bumping my shoulder as he passed. I didn't react to it, thinking I would provide an inspiring example of Christian forgiveness for all those kids on the buses.

I stood on the sand with my back to the biting wind and watched the buses back out. By the time they got to the underpass, their passengers had broken into a jubilant hymn. I realized my headache was back again.

CHAPTER TWENTY

It was 4:30 when I got back to my apartment. I made myself a drink and took a hot shower and was just drying off when the phone rang. Wrapping the towel around my waist, I went out to answer it.

"Asch?" a voice said urgently. "This is Haynes. Where the god-damn hell have you been? I've been trying to reach you since this morning. I must have called your answering service twenty times."

"I'm sorry, Mr. Haynes, but I haven't checked with the service yet. I've been out at the Word of God all day."

"Forget about the Word of God," he snapped. "Susan has been kidnaped."

The words picked me up and shook me. "How do you know?"

"We got a note this morning in the mail. They want $25,000 in small, unmarked bills. Otherwise they'll kill her."

"Who is 'they'?"

"How the hell am I supposed to know? They didn't sign their goddamn name."

"When is the payoff supposed to be made?"

"I don't know. They're supposed to call tonight and arrange it."

"Have you notified the police?"

"No," he said, his voice trembling with emotion. "The note says the house is being watched. If we call the police, they'll know and they'll kill her."

"I'll be right up," I said and hung up.

Twenty-five minutes later, I was ringing the Haynes doorbell. Robert Haynes answered the door. His face was seamed with tension, and his tiny eyes were wide open, giving him a strange, almost manic appearance.

He nodded me inside. As I walked past him, I got a strong, sweet-sour smell of Scotch. He was exuding it from his pores like musk, but he had none of the physical symptoms of drunkenness. In his present nervous state, he was probably metabolizing it faster than it could reach the psychomotor centers of his brain.

His eyes widened even more when he got a good look at my face and he said: "What the hell happened to you?"

"It's a long story. I'll explain later. Did the call come yet?"

"No," he said, closing the door. "I wish it would. It's this waiting that's killing me."

"Did the note give a time they would call?"

He shook his head. "All it said was tonight. It didn't mention a time."

I followed him into the living room where Mrs. Haynes was sitting on the couch. She had finally made it out of her robe and was casually dressed in a scarlet pullover and white slacks. She looked thinner than I had seen her last, her face even more pale and drawn. She nodded weakly as I came in. "Hello, Mr. Asch."

"Hello, Mrs. Haynes. How are you feeling?"

"I was feeling much better until this morning when this horrible mess began."

"I can imagine the strain you must be going through."

"I suppose it was inevitable that something like this would happen eventually, with the kind of people Susan persisted in associating with. I told her, but she wouldn't listen—" Her mouth closed over whatever else she was going to say and she swallowed it.

"Where's the note?" I asked her husband.

"I'll get it," he said, and went into the other room. He handed me a small, plain white dimestore envelope, the same kind that had been sent to Eric Gurney, except that this time, the address had been typed. The postmark indicated that it had been mailed the day before from Los Angeles. I lifted the flap and pulled out the two sheets of paper.

The stationery was the same type that had been used for the letter to Gurney, also.

Get $25,000 in small, unmarked bills. Twenties and fifties. Have ready if you ever want to see your daughter alive again. We will call you tonight and tell you where to drop the money.

If you get any bright ideas like calling the cops you can kiss your darling daughter good-bye. Your house is being watched so we'll know if you do.

The type was normal pica, but there were some distinguishing features on some of the letters. The e's, for example, were faded at the top, as were two of the feet on the m's, making the typewriter identifiable if it was ever found. I went on to the second note.

It was handwritten in ink, in the same sloping hand as the letter I had seen in Eric Gurney's office.

Dear Mother and Robert, Hi. I'm okay. They haven't hurt me or anything, but for God's sake please do exactly what these people want and I'll come home unharmed. Don't contact anybody, please. Otherwise, they say they'll kill me and they mean it. Wait until I come home before you try to notify the police. I love you both and miss you very much. I never realized how much until now.   Susan.

Across the bottom of the paper was Scotchtaped one torn half of Susan's driver's license.

I handed the sheets back to Haynes and said: "I think you should call the police and the FBI—"

"Can't you read?" Haynes said, shaking the letters at me. "They're going to kill her if we do. They're watching the house—"

"I doubt that they would jeopardize themselves by getting that close. Anybody trying to conduct a surveillance in this neighborhood would be making himself pretty conspicuous. They'd be running the risk of being identified."

"We still can't take the chance."

"Are you sure that's Susan's handwriting?"

"Of course I'm sure. Why?"

"Yesterday Eric Gurney received a note, also supposedly from Susan. But it didn't mention anything about any kidnaping. I'd like to compare the handwriting on both notes to make sure they match up."

"How do you know Eric received a letter?" Mrs. Haynes asked sharply.

"Because he called me and told me."

137

Her dark eyes calcified on my face. "How would he come to call you? How would he even know about you working for us?"

"Because I went to see him the day before," I said flatly.

Her cheeks flushed. "You saw him against my direct orders?"

"That's right. I felt it was necessary."

Her husband, possibly sensing that any further digging into the matter might unearth his own clandestine authorization of my visit to her ex-husband, stepped in and threw up his hands. "Look, let's forget about that right now. It's all water under the bridge. What's important is getting Susan back. What about this letter Eric got? What did it say?"

"That she'd rediscovered Jesus and was happy and not to send anybody to look for her. Gurney called me and wanted my advice about whether or not he should turn the note over to the police. He was worked up about the Farnsworth murder and was afraid Susan might be in some kind of danger from the Word of God, but he was also afraid to turn the note over to the cops because he didn't know if she might be involved in the thing in some way. He wanted to know what I knew before he made a move one way or the other."

"Did he give them the note?"

"Not to my knowledge. I told him to hold off until I had a chance to check out the Word of God. That's why you couldn't reach me today. I was out there trying to get a line on Susan."

He pounced on my words. "What did you find out?"

"Nothing. Sievers claims he hasn't seen her since she was taken out of there by you and Farnsworth. And I tend to believe him."

"Do you think he could have had something to do with this?" he asked, holding up the letter.

I shook my head. "There wouldn't be anything in it for him. He takes in the amount of that ransom note every month and a half. He'd have everything to lose and nothing to gain. Besides, if Susan had gone back to the Word of God and Sievers was planning to do something like this, he wouldn't have allowed her to mail a letter telling people where she was."

"But if Susan wasn't at the Word of God, why would she write that letter?"

"She never said specifically that she was. All she said was that she'd rediscovered Jesus. I assumed she was there because the letter was postmarked Fillmore."

138

"You think she could have fallen in with some other group of Jesus freaks?"

"It's possible. Personally, I think it's more likely that the letter was a phony."

"What do you mean, a phony?"

"Susan was seen a few days ago in the company of one John Lee Hunter. Hunter was the Satan's Warrior she was arrested with last year. He's also the Gypsy in that letter you and I found in her desk. Hunter got out of jail in July and had found out Susan was at the Word of God. He started visiting her there and then when she ran away last week, apparently she went looking for him. I managed to track down Hunter who admitted that Susan had been with him but said she'd left and gone back to the Word of God. Then he arranged to have some of his friends kick my face in. They would have done a first-class job of it if it hadn't been for a freak accident."

"I don't understand," Haynes said. "What this Hunter says corroborated Susan's letter to Eric—"

"That's right," I said. "And I think they were both lying."

"I still don't understand," Haynes said. "You think this Hunter and his friends are the ones who are holding Susan?"

"I don't know. Hunter's got a rap sheet as long as your arm. He wouldn't be averse to a little extortion, especially if the risks involved were low."

"What do you mean, 'if the risks involved were low'?"

"Would you be willing to prosecute your own daughter for extortion?"

"What the hell has that got to do with anything?"

"When Susan was seen with Hunter, she wasn't a prisoner by any stretch of the imagination. From the time she ran away from home the second time, at least up until Hunter dropped out of sight, they were living together."

"What are you suggesting, Mr. Asch?" Mrs. Haynes said, her eyes searching my face hawkishly. "That Susan is a part of a scheme to defraud us of $25,000?"

"It's a possibility I think it would be unwise to ignore," I said.

"That's ridiculous," Haynes lashed out. "Why would she do such a thing? What reason would she have?"

"Freedom. The money to buy it with. Revenge. You'd know better than I would."

"I can't believe she'd do something like that," he said, but his tone belied his words. He sounded as if he were frightened more by the spectre of Susan's possible involvement than by the fact of her life being in danger. "I think it's more likely that Hunter was telling the truth and that Susan fell in with some low-lifes who found out she had wealthy parents and decided to cash in on it. Or that this Hunter and his friends in that motorcycle gang started getting ideas about raking in some easy money. You said yourself that they're a bunch of criminal types anyway."

"You'd better hope that's not what happened," I said.

"Why?"

"Because Susan knows all of the Satan's Warriors. She rode with them, which means that she can identify them. If they decided to go in for a kidnaping, they could never turn her loose again. They'd have to kill her."

"Oh, God," he groaned. He spun on his heel and headed for the bar. "I need a drink."

He poured a double Scotch on the rocks for himself and Cynthia Haynes said to him: "I think I could use a drink, too, dear. My nerves are shot. A brandy."

Nobody asked me whether I wanted one. Servants weren't supposed to drink on duty.

Haynes brought a small snifter of brandy over to his wife and sat down on the edge of the couch with his Scotch. Cynthia took a tiny sip of brandy and sat back. "So what do you suggest we do, Mr. Asch?"

"What I suggested in the beginning—call the police."

"No," Haynes said forcefully. "I've said the police are out, and I mean they're out. Susan's life is at stake here. We can't take the chance that she might not be in danger. We've got to assume that she is."

"That's what I was assuming," I told him. "The police are experienced in handling situations like this. They could stake out the drop point for the payoff and—"

"No," he cut me off. "We can't risk it."

"My husband is right," Cynthia agreed. "We can't gamble with Susan's life."

"I think we should notify Eric Gurney about what's going on," I said. "He has a right to be in on any decision that may affect his daughter's life."

"He has no rights as far as Susan is concerned," she said, her face burning. "He abdicated his rights when he deserted his home for that, that whore of his."

I could see there was no way I could argue with her, so I dropped it. The end result of any confrontation between us would merely be my being fired. Although that thought was not exactly anathema to me, I didn't want to take on the burden of guilt I knew I would feel if I walked out now. By having had contact with the primary movers in Susan's life, I had picked up a strange attachment to the girl, the kind of pitying attachment one feels when one comes across a wounded animal that has been left for dead by sadistic hunters. It was a feeling of personal responsibility for being human and witnessing the cruelty and callousness of humanity. I turned to Robert Haynes. "You've got the money ready?"

"It's in the den."

"Let's take a look."

He set his drink down on the table next to the tray and led me into the den, where he squatted down behind the desk and inserted a key in the door of a wooden cabinet. He opened the cabinet door, revealing a steel safe, and began working on the combination. He turned the dial to the last number and wrenched the handle and pulled open the door. I bent down to take a look.

The two shelves in the safe were filled with stacks of twenties and fifties, all arranged in neat bundles and wrapped in paper bands. I straightened up and he closed the door again and spun the dial.

"When the call comes through," I said, "I'll use the extension in here." He nodded, and I said: "I'd also lay off the booze if I were you. You're going to need complete control of all your faculties to get through this thing. It would be a hell of a note if you got pinched for drunk driving while you were on your way to make the drop."

His face flushed. I turned my back on him and walked out of the room, leaving him there to think about it. He followed me out into the living room and sat down in his chair, but made no movement toward the glass of Scotch that sat on the table in front of him.

We sat in silence, the tension in the room thickening with the twilight. The only break came when Maria came in to replenish the supply of coffee and sandwiches. Finally, Mrs. Haynes, her face peaked and wan, stood up. "I don't feel well. I'm afraid the strain of the last few days has been too much for me. I'm going to lie down for awhile."

"Why don't you take a Valium and try to get some rest, dear?" Haynes said solicitously. "There's nothing you can do anyway."

"Get me up if anything happens."

We both assured her we would, and she went down the hall. The stuffiness of the house was starting to make me drowsy, and I told Haynes I was going to get some air.

I opened the sliding glass door and went out by the pool and sat down in one of the patio chairs. The city was on fire beyond the darkness of the hills, a magnificent blanket of lights, and that, and the cool evening air, partially revived me. I rested my head against the back of the chair and closed my eyes. I hoped Haynes wouldn't follow me out. My headache was starting to come back, and I didn't want to have to confront his gnawing anxieties again until I had to. After five minutes passed, I guessed he wasn't coming and I started to relax.

I don't know if I dozed off or not, but my eyes snapped open to the ringing of the phone.

Haynes was already at the phone and was about to pick it up when I grabbed his arm. "Let it ring twice more. That'll give me time to get into the den."

I ran down the hall and got to the phone as the second ring sounded. I lifted the receiver gently off its cradle, keeping my hand over the mouthpiece.

"Hello?"

"Is this Haynes?" a raspy voice said. The voice was muffled, as if the man was talking through a handkerchief, but it wasn't disguised enough for me not to recognize it.

"This is Haynes."

"You got the money?"

"Yes."

"Okay. Now shut up and listen. Put the money in a suitcase and put it in the trunk of your Mercedes. Start now. Drive out Pacific Coast Highway to Trancas Canyon. There's a closed drive-in restaurant there. Pull in and park by the phone booth at the corner of the lot and wait. I'll call you and tell you where to go from there. Come alone and don't get any cute ideas; otherwise, the girl is fucking dead. Got me?"

"Is Susan all right?" Haynes said, his voice almost a whine.

"She's fine, but she won't be if you don't do like you're told."

"How do I know you're telling the truth? Let me talk to her."

"Just do like I fucking tell you, Haynes," the other voice said angrily.

"Listen—" Haynes tried to say, but he was talking to a dial tone. I hung up and went back into the living room.

Haynes was still holding the phone, staring at it as if he were in a daze. He looked up when I came in. "You heard?"

"Yeah, I heard."

"He sounded like he meant business. He sounded like he'd kill her without a second thought."

"You were talking to John Hunter."

That startled him out of his daze. He looked down at the receiver in his hand as if surprised to see it there, then put it down. "You're sure it was Hunter?"

"I've talked to him on the phone and in person. His voice isn't one you'd mistake easily."

"What can we do?"

"Call the police. Tell them to meet us at Trancas Canyon."

"No," he said, shaking his head. "I told you I won't take that kind of a risk with Susan's life, and I meant it. And I'm tired of your insinuations about Susan being in on this."

"Well, if she isn't, the only chance we've got of getting her back alive is to find her before Hunter decides it's time to get rid of her."

"How do we know he hasn't already? He might have already killed her. Maybe that's why he wouldn't let me talk to her."

"I doubt that. If it's a serious kidnaping attempt, he'd want to keep her alive until he got his money, just in case you were reluctant to pay and he needed to use her to apply some leverage."

His shoulders slumped forward and he said: "What are we going to do?"

"Just what he told you to do. You're going to take the money and go to that drive-in and wait for that call. When you get it, you're going to write down the instructions he gives you on a piece of paper and leave it on the ledge in the phone booth. That

143

way, if anybody's watching the phone booth, it'll look like you're alone."

He looked puzzled. "But I *will* be alone—"

"No, you won't. I'll be right behind you."

"But he said he'll kill her if I don't come alone—"

"If he's going to kill her, he's going to kill her anyway. Remember that."

"All right, all right," he agreed nervously, and I started for the door. "Where are you going?"

"Back to my apartment," I said. "I left something there. I'll catch up with you at the beach."

CHAPTER TWENTY-ONE

I drove to my apartment and got my .45 auto out of the bedside drawer, loaded a clip, and left again. I took the freeway to the beach and drove through the tunnel that opened onto the coast highway. I followed the lights of the beach, past seafood restaurants and steak houses that lined the rocky shoreline like the hulls of giant beached schooners, past the huge white houses of the Malibu Colony, souvenirs of a wealth and a sweet decadence long gone. Then the lights went out and the land became dark, only the white foam of the breakers showing where the sea ended and the land began.

I drove past Point Dune, past the white sands of Zuma Beach, toward Trancas. I saw the boarded-up drive-in ahead on the right, as dark and desolate as my thoughts. There was no sign of Haynes' Mercedes.

I pulled in and parked next to the phone booth. The note was there on the shelf. *Up Trancas Canyon Road to Mulholland. Stop, leave money at bush by crossroads.*

I stuck the note in my pocket and drove out of the parking lot, up the hill. The road wound into the jagged gash of canyon in steep, unbanked curves. I drove fast, ignoring the squealing protest from my tires, keeping my foot in it all the way. After a couple of miles I caught sight of the Mercedes' taillights and flashed my high beams as I swung out and went ahead. I kept on the accelerator, and soon his headlights disappeared in my rearview mirror. By the time I reached Mulholland I figured I had a good five minutes on him. I slowed down and scanned the side of the road as I sailed through the intersection. Three-tenths of a mile past the intersection, the road curved around a rocky bend. Past that, a dirt fire road cut a path down into a scrubby ravine. I pulled off the pavement and drove a little way down the fire road, then turned around and doused my lights. I got out of the car and walked back up to the pavement, around the bend in the road. The dropoff point was visible from there. I found some cover from which to watch and wait.

A few minutes later, Haynes' Mercedes came up the hill and stopped in the intersection. His door opened, and he stepped out into the road with the suitcase. He walked around in front of the car, breaking the beams of his headlights, and started across the road. He looked both ways, set the suitcase down behind a large bush, then went back to the car and drove off.

He passed me on the road without seeing me, and I watched his taillights disappear around the curve in the road. Then I turned back toward the bush.

A few minutes later, I heard the sound of a motorcycle. A single headlight came up the road from the direction of the beach. I could hear the rider rev the engine as he downshifted and the bike came to a stop in front of the bush. The rider got off and put the kickstand down on the bike, then went over to the bush and picked up the suitcase. He stood by the side of the road for a second, motionless, like a wild animal sniffing the wind for the scent of a predator. Then he got back on the bike and took off. As the bike roared past me, I got a good look at the rider. It was Hunter.

I sprinted back to the car and got in. I drove with lights for awhile, to try to make up for the time I lost getting to the car, then turned them off. The moon hadn't come up yet, and the road was dark. Around several curves I lost the pavement and dipped off onto the dirt shoulder, my tires squealing loudly as I yanked the wheel to correct the drift.

I caught sight of Hunter's taillight and stayed just close enough to keep him in sight. The road twisted tortuously into the mountains and then began dropping. Then there was a sign that said Cornell, and we passed a cluster of dark buildings. A mile past that, he swung his bike off the pavement onto a dirt road that led through a clump of scrub oak. I followed.

The road led up to a small, wooden house set back from the road. I parked down from the house and got out my gun and pulled back the slide, injecting a bullet into the chamber.

A cold breeze blew in my face as I got out of the car, cooling the beads of perspiration on my forehead. A car swished by on the pavement, its headlights sweeping the dirt road. An owl screamed somewhere in the thickness of the trees.

Hunter's bike stood alone by the side of the house. I ran for it in a half-crouch. I scrambled behind the machine, keeping it between me and the house and paused there, listening intently for some sound of alarm from inside the house. I could hear the sound of muffled voices, but although I couldn't make out what they were saying, there didn't seem to be any alarm in them. Then I heard somebody laugh and relaxed a little.

I put the .45 down and got out my pocket knife. Then I cut the fuel line on the bike and pulled off the sparkplug wires, throwing them over my head into the bushes. Then, keeping low, I went around the bike to the wall. There was a window a few yards away. A slice of light spilled from between its half-closed curtains onto the ground. I edged along the wall until I was underneath the sill and peeked in.

Hunter was standing in the center of the tiny living room with his back to the window, talking to someone I couldn't see. The suitcase was open on the couch in front of him. He suddenly grew silent and stared down at it. I couldn't see the expression on his face, but I was sure it was probably one of awe. He dipped his hands down into the case and came up with two fistfuls of money, then opened his fingers and let the green bundles drop back into the case.

I left the window and made my way to the back of the house and peeked around the corner. There was a small cement porch back there and next to it, a row of battered trash cans, overflowing with garbage. I ran for them.

Crouched behind the piles of stinking garbage, I surveyed the house. I must have been behind the kitchen. A screen door opened onto the cement porch, and there was another door behind that. I skittered along the ground on all fours, crab-fashion, and stayed low while I tried the door. It creaked as I pulled it open. The wooden door behind it had glass panes in its upper half. I stuck my head up over the edge and looked into the kitchen. The lights were off inside, but there was enough light coming in from the other room to let me see that the room was empty. I tried the handle of the door; it was open.

I slipped inside and shut the door quietly. The narrow kitchen smelled of bacon grease and rotting garbage. Hunter must have lived in garbage. I tiptoed to the open doorway leading into the living room and stopped there.

My heart was pounding. I didn't seem to be able to take in enough oxygen to fill my lungs. I took a deep breath and was about to step out when I heard Hunter's voice call out from around the corner: "Hurry up and get your ass in gear and let's get the fuck out of here."

Footsteps clomped heavily toward me. I sucked in a breath and held it, cocking back my hand with the .45 in it, and waited. His silhouette partially blocked out the light of the doorway, and I swung the .45 across his face. His feet went out from under him, and he went down like a 200-pound sack of sand, without uttering a sound. I bent down and examined him. The gun opened up a large gash along the side of his chin. It was bleeding freely, but I figured he would be all right. I stepped over him and into the living room.

The room was small, shabby, and incredibly stuffy. The suitcase was still open on the couch, undisturbed. I stopped and listened. There was an open door on the other side of the couch. I could hear somebody moving around behind it. I went toward it quietly and pushed the door open slowly.

A girl was bent over a cheap wooden bureau pulling clothes out of its drawers and tossing them on a swayback bed. She straightened up as I came in, but didn't turn around until I was completely in the room. "I'll be ready in just a sec. Hold on, will y—SHIT!"

Her mouth dropped open when she saw I wasn't Hunter. She looked older than her graduation picture, thinner, dissipated, hollow-eyed, but there was no mistaking that blond halo.

"Hello, Susan."

"Who the hell are you?" she asked frantically. "Where's Gypsy?"

"I'm afraid he's indisposed at the moment."

"Where is he?" She looked past me into the living room, her eyes registering panic. "GYPSY!"

"He can't hear you. He's out cold."

Her expression changed suddenly from one of panic to one of defiance, and she thrust her chin out at me. "Who are you—a pig? I didn't think good old Robert would have the fucking nerve to call the pigs. I guess I sort of misjudged things."

"Not necessarily," I said. "I'm not a cop. I'm a private investigator your stepfather hired to find you."

Her eyes widened in surprise. "Gypsy said—" but then she cut herself off.

"Said what? That he'd arranged to have me put in intensive care? He tried, but he fucked up. As a matter of fact, he fucked up all down the line. He didn't even pull off the road once between the money drop and here to see if anybody was following him."

"Shit," she said, throwing a disgusted look into the other room and sitting down hard on the bed. "Jesus goddamn fucking Christ."

"You cooked this whole scheme up, didn't you? Somehow I think it was a little over your boyfriend's mental capacity. And that letter you sent to your father to try to throw everybody off —as ridiculous as that was, it showed too much subtlety for old Gypsy."

She sat glaring at me like a trapped animal, not saying anything.

"Why'd you do it?"

"Because I had it coming," she said bitterly. "They owe me."

"Where were you going to go with all that money?"

Her eyes darted around the room. "Anywhere. Away from this fucking place. Away from *them*."

"You mean Haynes and your mother?"

She nodded.

"You're eighteen. Legally you could have gone anywhere you wanted. You didn't have to pull this kind of a stunt."

She looked up. Her face was transformed, twisted into an ugly glare. "Like I said, they owe me. Besides, what would they use the money for? Cynthia would just spend it on tranquilizers and more trips to her fucking shrink that wouldn't do any good. And good old lecherous Robert—all he'd use it for would be to buy more Scotch so he could get plastered and pass out." She looked down at the gun in my hand and said: "What are you going to do?"

"To you? Nothing. That'll be up to your mother and stepfather —and the police."

She smiled. "The pigs can't do anything. Dear Cynthia and

149

Robert wouldn't press charges against their darling daughter. They love her too much."

"Maybe not," I said. "But the cops don't need anybody to press charges in a murder case."

The smile vanished from her lips and she squinted at me. "What murder? I don't know anything about any murder."

"The murder of Larry Farnsworth," I said. "Your big mistake was turning your animal boyfriend loose to do his thing, honey. He belongs in a cage. He's got no sense of proportion at all. The first person who comes around asking questions about you, he tries to stomp him into the ground to get him out of the way. Like me. But he went a little overboard on Farnsworth. And then, to cover your tracks, you tried to set up the Word of God to take the blame for both the murder and the kidnaping. Communal life must have really left you with a bad taste in your mouth."

She jumped up off the bed, her fists tightly clenched. "We never laid a hand on Farnsworth. We never even knew he was looking for me until you laid it on Gypsy last night—"

"Save it for the cops," I said, holding up my hand. "They can try to sort it out. It's their baby now."

"You're not taking me to any motherfucking pigs," she said, backing away from me.

"I don't intend taking you anywhere," I said and meant it. The thought of trying to control ninety pounds of fighting fury on the freeway didn't appeal to me somehow. Besides, I realized I was sick and tired of the case and everybody involved in it. All I wanted was out. I turned and walked into the living room. I tucked the gun into my waistband and closed the suitcase and picked it up and started for the door.

I had my hand on the knob when she called out: "Wait!"

I turned around. She was standing in the bedroom doorway, watching the suitcase in my hand anxiously. "Listen, I'll give you half the bread. Man, that's twelve thousand five hundred bucks. Nobody'll ever know. You could just say you couldn't find us, you know? Listen, you could have a good time on twelve thousand bucks."

"Thanks for offering me half of what I've already got all of—that is, if I wanted it. It just so happens that I don't. Good-bye, Susan."

I turned and opened the door. Out of the corner of my eye,

I saw her move quickly around the edge of the couch. I turned my head to see what she was going to do, which was a mistake. I heard a rustling sound coming through the doorway but too late to do anything about it.

Something hard and heavy smashed against the side of my face. My neck went loose and my head sagged against the doorway. I tried to lift it up to see, but another blow came down on the top of my head, and I slid down the wall. I was tumbling down the well again, head over heels, into darkness.

There was no way to tell how long I had been out. I rolled over and opened my eyes, trying to gether up all the pieces of my mind that I could find. Cool night air blew in through the open doorway and gently brushed my cheek. I listened for a sound, but could hear nothing but the indifferent chirping of the crickets outside. With a monumental effort, I sat up. That was when I saw that I was not alone.

Susan Gurney hadn't left. She was sprawled across the shabby couch, her face a mass of blood, the blond halo stained red. Blood was everywhere, soaking the front of her white T-shirt, splattered on the wall behind her, across the couch, in dark stains on the floor. Something in me went limp and my stomach turned sour, but I fought down the nausea and struggled to my feet.

I went cautiously toward the kitchen. Hunter was gone.

CHAPTER TWENTY-TWO

Two hours later I was in a small, sterile room in the back of the sheriff's substation in Malibu, going over my story for the sixth time with a long-faced detective sergeant named Kleinst. Kleinst had heavy, dark eyebrows and a neatly-clipped mustache. He listened to my narrative all the way through, then tossed the pencil he was holding down on top of the desk.

"So you think Hunter woke up, then went out the back door of the house and around front, hit you over the head, and then killed the girl and split with the money."

"I didn't say that. I didn't see who hit me. It could have been Hunter. It could have been somebody else."

"But you say there was nobody else there at the time—"

"Nobody that I saw, anyway."

He nodded. "You disabled Hunter's bike. It was still parked outside when we got there. So how did he make it out of there?"

"That's a good question."

"How about an answer?"

"I don't have one. I guess you'd have to postulate a third man, somebody who knew about what was happening and who took off with Hunter. Unless Hunter took the suitcase and started hoofing it, which isn't very likely. The keys to my car were in my pocket. He could have easily taken them."

"Did you see any other bikes around besides his?"

"I told you, no."

He thought about that and picked up the Styrofoam cup full of coffee that sat on the table in front of him.

"You hear anything while you were inside, like the sound of somebody driving up, for instance?"

"No."

"Did the girl mention anything about anybody else besides her and Hunter being in on the extortion scheme?"

I shook my head.

"What about that note to her father? What was that all about?"

"She didn't come right out and say it, but I'm sure she was playing her father for a chump. She didn't think he'd tell anybody about it, at least until after he got news of the kidnaping. And then, while the cops were wasting time interrogating members from the Word of God, she and Hunter would be long gone to parts unknown. They obviously didn't count on me stepping into the picture and lousing things up for them by turning up witnesses who'd seen them together a few days before the kidnaping. But by that time both letters had already been sent, so the only thing they could do was try to get me out of the way as fast as possible by putting me in the hospital."

He took a sip of the coffee and then grimaced sourly into the cup as if it had betrayed him. He put the cup back down on the desk and said: "Okay. You say it didn't sound to you as if Hunter and the girl were arguing—"

"That's right. From the way it sounded, they were just getting ready to leave together."

"It seems pretty funny that they'd go to all the trouble of planning this whole thing together. Then suddenly he'd decide he wanted all the money for himself and kill her."

"I never said he did kill her—"

"Then who did?" he asked, staring at me levelly. "Somebody sure as hell killed her. And did a pretty messy job of it, too. If it *was* Hunter who hit you over the head and killed the girl, why did he leave you alive, knowing you could point a finger at him and send him to Folsom for life?"

"I don't know, sergeant. It's hard to think right now. Maybe I'll get it sorted out later, but I've been hit on the head too many times in the last two days to be thinking clearly."

He came forward in his chair and leaned both forearms on the table, watching me intently. "This story of yours is pretty muddled in my mind, too, Asch. A girl is supposedly kidnaped, and you don't call the police—"

"I told you I wanted to. My client refused to let me."

"But he let you go against, for all he knew, the entire Satan's Warriors gang single-handed."

153

"After that call came through, there wasn't time to do anything else."

He leaned back and threw me a disgusted look. "Well, I hope he's satisfied. Both of you."

"Look, sergeant, I told you, I didn't have any choice—"

He stabbed a finger at me and said: "Don't give me any of that shit, mister. You had a choice. You've been watching too many B movies. You're letting all this James Bond shit go to your head. You should have quit and called the police. That was your choice, mister. A purely moral one. But you wanted to go out and play hero, and so now we've got a girl down at the morgue without a face."

I had felt bad enough before he had started on me. Now I felt rotten. "Are you through with me?"

"For now," he said, his voice hard. "But don't go anywhere where I can't get hold of you in five minutes."

I stood up. "How about my gun?"

"I think I'll hold onto it for awhile."

"On what grounds?"

"You don't have a permit to carry it, do you?"

"I don't have to. I don't carry it."

"You were carrying it tonight."

"It wasn't concealed."

"And I'm supposed to take your word on that."

"How long are you going to keep it?"

"Until the autopsy reports come in."

I stared at him. "You've got to be kidding."

"I'm not kidding," he said. "I'm not kidding at all."

"What would my motive be for murdering the girl, sergeant?"

He picked up the pen again and held it in both hands. His face had hardened into a cement mask. "Twenty-five thousand dollars is a lot of money."

"Shit," I said with as much contempt as I could muster and left.

On the way home I went over the events at the murder scene in my mind, trying to dredge up something that would give me a clue to what had happened; but the picture I got was fuzzy. As soon as I reached my apartment, I phoned Haynes. He answered.

"Hello?" His voice was dull and heavy.

"Haynes? This is Asch."

There was a pause. "Goddamn you," the voice said, clogged with emotion. "I'm going to have your ass for this." Then I was listening to the steady, monotonous buzz of the dial tone. I replaced the receiver gently and went into the kitchen. I poured myself a slug of bourbon, downed it, and poured another one. After the fourth one, I was ready not to remember for awhile. I got undressed and went to bed.

I dreamed I was in a courtroom on trial for my life. The jury was 12 faceless women with blood-soaked hair. They pronounced me guilty as charged, and I woke up crying. Even though there was nobody there to see me, I felt ashamed of my tears and went into the bathroom to wash my face.

CHAPTER TWENTY-THREE

I was brought slowly out of an exhausted sleep by the sound of a buzzer. I reached over and hit my alarm clock, but the buzzer kept up insistently, at irregular but more frequent intervals. It took me a full half-minute to realize it was my doorbell. I got up groggily and went to the door and asked who was there.

"Kleinst," a voice said.

I said just a minute and pulled on a pair of pants and went back to the door. He was wearing the same gray suit and paisley tie he had had on the night before, and the same distant look in his eyes, except more so. I guessed some of it was due to fatigue. He looked as if he had slept very little last night, if at all.

"What do you want?" I asked coldly.

"I came to return your gun."

Most of the animosity I had felt for him last night had dissipated. But because of the guilt that was attached to it, I was reluctant to let it go completely. "Okay."

I held out my hand and he brought the gun from underneath his coat and handed it to me. "I'd also like to talk to you."

"Since this case started, it seems like all I've been doing is talking to cops. And the intellectual level of the conversations has been uniformly low."

He set his jaw against the remark but let it go by. We stood staring at each other for a few seconds, then he said: "Can I come in?"

I shrugged and pulled the door open, and he walked past me into the apartment. He stood in the center of the room, looking at the disheveled bed clothes, trying to figure out where to sit. I motioned toward the breakfast table. "Welcome to my tortilla flat, sergeant. Sit down at the table."

"Thanks," he said and sat down.

"I was just going to make some coffee. You want some?"

"If you're going to make it anyway, that would be nice. Don't go to any special bother for me, though."

I went into the kitchen and put on the kettle, then slipped a paper filter into my cone brewer and started to measure out the coffee.

"I'm sorry if I woke you up," he said apologetically. "I didn't think you'd be sleeping this late."

"What time is it?"

"Quarter to ten."

"I normally don't. I had a rotten night's sleep last night, and I'm tired."

He unbuttoned his coat and leaned back in his chair. "I talked to Al Herrera this morning."

He waited for me to say something, and when I didn't, he went on. "He said you were a pretty straight guy and that you've helped him out on quite a few things in the past."

"Really? What else did he say?"

"I told him I was pretty rough on you last night. He said I should ease up."

"Is that why you decided to give me my gun back?"

"Partially, maybe. I've known Al for a long time. I respect his judgment. He's a good cop."

I studied his face and said: "I didn't ask Al to put a word in for me."

"I know. He saw the report this morning and asked me about it."

The kettle started to whistle. I took it off the flame and began pouring the hot water into the cone. "So what's the other part of the 'partially'?" He threw me a confused look, and I said: "You said Al was partially the reason you gave me my gun back. What's the other part?"

"The autopsy was done early this morning on the girl. I haven't got the official report yet, but I talked to the pathologist who did the job."

"And?"

"The girl was shot to death. They took four slugs out of her—.38's."

"Larry Farnsworth was shot with a .38."

157

"I've already sent the bullets to ballistics to see if I can get a match-up," he said.

"What about her face? It was pulverized—"

"Before she was shot, she was beaten severely with a blunt object. The bullets are what killed her, though."

"What kind of blunt object? You have any idea?"

"The pathologist said it looked like it might have been the barrel of a heavy revolver, but that's just a guess."

I watched the coffee drain and stifled a yawn. "How do you take it?" I asked him as I got two cups out from the cupboard and poured coffee into both.

"Black."

I handed him the cup, then went to the icebox and put some milk in mine. I spooned out some sugar from the bowl on the drainboard and took a seat opposite him at the table.

"This is good coffee," he said. "Believe me, after living on that rotgut shit at the station, I appreciate good coffee."

"Thanks. Glad you like it."

"I talked to your principal this morning," he said, after a pause. "He's putting all the blame on you. He said you forced him into going along with the idea of trying to tail the pickup man back to the girl."

"That's true, I did, but only if the pickup man was Hunter. I also told him he should call the cops, or didn't he mention that?"

"He said you made a half-hearted suggestion."

"Shit. Have you talked to Eric Gurney?"

"Yeah, I talked to him."

"What did he have to say?"

"Haynes had already called him and given him his version of the story. When I talked to him, he didn't speak of you with any particular fondness. You're not a very popular guy right now with anybody."

"Even with myself." I put my cup down on the table and said: "I still can't see a motive for Hunter, why he would have suddenly decided to kill the girl."

"Maybe he was planning it all along," he offered. "Maybe he was just biding his time until the payoff, just in case Haynes didn't come through at first, and he needed to prove she was alive. If Hunter killed Farnsworth and the girl knew about it, maybe he just figured it would be safer to eliminate her altogether."

"If it was that premeditated, why did he bother to beat the shit out of her? And like you said last night, why did he leave me alive to identify him?"

He didn't say anything. He just watched me from over the rim of his cup.

"Have you figured out how Hunter got out of there yet?"

"There's only one way he could have. Somebody had to have been in on it with him and driven him out."

"Did you find any tire tracks by the house?"

"The ground is too hard. It's like a real hard clay."

"How about fingerprints?"

"There were hundreds of sets in the house. It'll be quite a while before we identify them all, if we ever do. We found a couple of bloody prints in the kitchen that look promising, but we haven't been able to match them up yet."

"Got any ideas who might have been the accomplice?"

He blinked, then opened his tired eyes wide to stretch them. "We're in the process of running down all the Satan's Warriors now. We've got one in custody—the guy who was leasing the house. Delbert Ferguson III, if you believe that one. His gang name is Dirty Delbert because he's so fucking filthy. I don't think the son of a bitch has taken a bath in a year. He really stinks. I don't know how anybody could rent their house to him, but the owner did. He says old Delbert is a good tenant, always pays his rent on time and never causes him any trouble. If he doesn't want to take a bath, that's his business."

"What about this Delbert character?"

He shrugged. "He's got a pretty strong alibi for the time of the murder. He says he spent the night in a bar over in Pacoima. He gave us a dozen names of people who saw him there and so far, they're checking out."

"Where did you pick him up?"

"At the house. He came cruising in this morning around three o'clock, big as life."

"Did he know about the extortion plot?"

"He says no. Says Hunter came to him a couple of days ago and said he'd been evicted from his apartment and asked if he and the girl could stay at his place for a couple of days. Delbert told them Okay. He says he wouldn't have let them stay if he'd known what they were up to."

"Do you believe him?"

"I don't know," he said. "All I know is that I don't have enough to hold him on, so we'll probably cut him loose this afternoon."

"Did he say if he ever saw Hunter and the girl get into any arguments while he was around?"

"He says they had a few squabbles but nothing major. And nothing physical."

I nodded and pointed to his cup. "Some more coffee?"

"No, no thanks. I'm just on my way home to try to grab some z's. I just stopped by to give you your gun back and find out if maybe you remembered something about last night that might be significant."

"I'm afraid not. I don't even think it's a case of remembering. I don't think there is anything to remember."

He nodded and then quickly said: "Look, Asch, I was pretty hot last night, and I probably said some things I shouldn't have. I apologize for that. That doesn't mean I don't think you weren't a jerk for doing what you did."

"I was a jerk. I admit it. I spent a lot of last night sitting up trying to analyze my own motives for what I did. Maybe you were right, maybe I was trying to grandstand, I don't know. I haven't come up with any answers yet. Any final ones, anyway. But you'll be the first to know as soon as I do."

He smiled wearily and stood up. "Okay. If you do happen to remember something, give me a call. And thanks again for the coffee."

"Anytime," I said. "Feel free to drop on in for a cup."

"I'll do that."

I followed him to the door. He pulled it open, then turned around as if he had forgotten something. "By the way, what blood type are you?"

The question took me off balance, but after a few seconds I gathered my thoughts together and said: "O, why?"

"Not A, huh?"

"No. Why?"

"We found some A blood at the house. The girl's group was O, too."

"It could be Hunter's. He was bleeding pretty good from that cut on his face—"

He shook his head, cutting me off. "This blood didn't come from any facial cut. There was too much of it."

"What do you think it means?"

He raised his eyebrows vaguely. "I don't know. If you think of anything, be sure and call. Thanks again for the coffee."

I stood listening to his heavy footsteps trudge down the outside stairs, then went back to the stove and poured myself another cup of coffee. I let it turn cold while I debated with myself whether I should try to call Eric Gurney and give him my side of it. In the end I rejected the idea, deciding that it wasn't exactly a tactful time to impose on his grief just to try to justify my own actions.

I started to feel restless. The thought of remaining any longer in that tiny wallboard box suddenly became intolerable. I threw on some clothes and went down to the car.

I got on the freeway and drove, not knowing where I was heading, just driving. I wound up at the Redondo Beach pier. I had breakfast there at a coffee shop overlooking the breakers, then walked along the beach, watching the birds and the afternoon sun play on the water. None of it helped.

It was a quarter to four by the time I got back to the apartment. I made myself a drink and stretched out on my unmade bed. The combination of the drink and the lack of sleep the night before made me drowsy. I must have dozed off because the next thing I was aware of was that the phone was ringing and my clock said 6:15.

"Hello?"

"Asch?"

"Right."

"What's the matter? You sound funny. This is Kleinst."

"Oh, hello, sergeant. I must have fallen asleep."

"Shit, is that all you do—sleep? Listen, we've found Hunter."

I bolted upright in bed. "When?"

"A couple of hours ago."

"Where?"

"About five miles from the house, off Mulholland. Somebody did a pretty sloppy job of burying him."

My thoughts were racing now, and I had to back up to what he had just said. "What did you say?"

"He's dead, Asch. It looks as if his accomplice got greedy. His body is at the medical examiner's now. I want you to go down there and make a positive identification, just to make it official that the man you saw at the house last night was really Hunter."

"I'll be down there in half an hour," I said and hung up.

CHAPTER TWENTY-FOUR

Kleinst was waiting outside the double glass doors when I reached the County Hospital. He looked revitalized, as if he had made it home and gotten those few hours of sleep he had been talking about.

We greeted each other, and I asked anxiously: "So tell me how they found him."

"Some hippie was out hiking around the area this morning with his dog, and suddenly his dog started to go nuts and dig. The grave was shallow. It didn't take long for the dog to come up with a foot."

"Hunter was your A blood?"

"That's what it looks like."

"How far off the road was the body buried?"

He shrugged. "Maybe fifty yards. Not far. Hunter was a pretty heavy boy. Whoever did it probably didn't want to carry him very far."

"You'd think he'd have picked a more isolated spot to bury him—"

"From the looks of things, the guy was in a hurry. He was probably excited and wanted to ditch the body as soon as he could," he said indifferently, then turned toward the doors behind him. "Let's go in and take a look."

We went into the modern, sterile lobby whose freshly waxed linoleum floor looked like something Gene Kelly would have been proud to dance on.

The doors of the elevator slid open and we started to step in, but I was surprised to find myself facing John Hunter's mother and her husband, Muller. A large, bulky man who was obviously a detective had his hand on Mrs. Muller's elbow. She had her head down, her face buried in a handkerchief. Her husband was standing off to one side of her, a look of annoyed disdain stamped clearly on his face as he watched his wife's shoulders heave in convulsive sobs.

The woman looked at me as she stepped off the elevator; her mascara-streaked eyes gave no sign that they recognized me. She and the detective went on past us, but Muller lagged back a few steps and grabbed my arm when he came even with us. "Where's my thirty bucks?" he whispered.

"What thirty bucks?"

"Listen," he growled, "don't try to give me any of that shit. You owe me thirty bucks for getting you in touch with that scumbag son of hers."

"That's funny. Hunter never mentioned you. And I guess it's a little late to ask him about it now."

"Why you son of a bitch, I'll—"

Whatever he was going to say, he glanced at Kleinst and squelched it, then strode angrily down the hall after his wife.

"What was that all about?" Kleinst asked as we stepped into the elevator. I told him briefly, and he looked intrigued. "I spent a half hour with that asshole this morning, and he never mentioned that little tidbit. I'm going to have to ask him a few more questions real soon." He smiled impishly. "And that's going to be a pleasure. I'm going to make that bastard sweat."

We stepped out into a yellow corridor whose overhead lighting was so intense that it almost hurt the eyes. "This way," Kleinst said, waving a hand off to our right.

A sickeningly sweet odor filled the corridor, like the smell of roasting pork except more pungent. I mentioned it to Kleinst.

"That's from the fire. There was a fire in a flophouse downtown. They just brought in some of the bodies a few hours ago. Even with the air-conditioning it takes a long time to get rid of the smell."

White-jacketed attendants moved through the hall. Along one wall, two white enamel tables stood silently, with their loads waiting to be processed. On one of the tables the sheet had been pulled back, revealing a big black man with parts of his face missing.

"Knife fight," Kleinst said, glancing casually down at the black man's face. "In here."

He pushed through some swinging doors at the end of the corridor. I followed him into a white room where we were met by a tall, thin-faced doctor dressed in a rubber apron, whom Kleinst introduced as Dr. Cranston. Cranston offered a reluctant smile and a bony, nicotine-stained hand, then he led the way through another set of doors.

The walls in the room were lined with rows of stainless steel refrigerator doors. The doctor walked over to one of them and pulled it open. He pulled back the sheet from the drawer, and I looked down on what was left of Hunter's face. I say what was left of it because somebody had done a good job of hacking it into a mass of unrecognizable hamburger. Deep lacerations covered the forehead, and across the eyes, the nose was split apart. Large pieces of ragged flesh hung loose from the cheeks and mouth. There were two black bullet holes in his chest, one right about where the heart would have been.

"Jesus," I said, wanting to turn away but unable to, my eyes somehow fastened to the mutilated corpse.

"This the man you saw with Susan Gurney?"

I nodded. "Yes," I said, but my throat had dried up, and my voice was barely audible.

"I want to show you something very interesting," Kleinst said, his voice betraying nothing but that: mild interest. He could have been talking about a lump of putty. He pulled the sheet down farther, uncovering the corpse to the knees. Whoever had done the hatchet job on Hunter's face had duplicated it on his genitals.

Before I had a chance to say anything, Kleinst turned to the doctor and asked: "What kind of an instrument do you think made these wounds?"

"It's hard to say. We'll know more when we do the autopsy. I wouldn't want to speculate about it now."

Kleinst nodded. "Would you say the mutilation was done before or after he was dead?"

"Like I say," the doctor said, hedging, "I wouldn't want to theorize at this point, sergeant. I'll know more when I cut him open—"

"I'm not asking you for any commitment," Kleinst said, his voice now showing traces of irritation. "All I'm asking for is an educated guess."

"It wouldn't be professional of me to speculate on something like that at this point," the doctor said, his voice calm and steady. "I should have something for you by morning."

"All right, all right," Kleinst said, holding up his hands. Then he turned and went toward the doors.

When we got back into the hall, he said: "Trying to get anything out of that son of a bitch is like trying to get blood from a turnip."

"What do you think about that mutilation?"

"Whoever did it either hated Hunter or himself a lot," he said. "For his sake, I hope the poor bastard was already dead when the guy started."

"Got any ideas as to how it happened?"

"Some," he said, then he fell silent.

"Want to share them?"

He walked to the elevator, looking down at his feet, lost in thought, then said: "I think one of Hunter's good biker buddies heard about what he was planning to do—either he was in on it or Hunter shot his mouth off about it—and he decided to pull a rip-off. He came in, hit you over the head, killed the girl and Hunter and took Hunter's body with him. That's why he didn't bother to kill you. You were the witness who could testify to Hunter having been in the house with the girl. He knew you'd tell us and that we'd be spending all our time trying to track down a dead man. We still would be if it hadn't have been for that hippie and his dog."

The elevator arrived, and he motioned me in.

"It seems like he would have chosen a better site for a grave if he was planning the whole thing that far in advance—"

"Maybe he wasn't," Kleinst suggested. "Maybe he just planned to kill them both and take the money, but your being on the scene changed the whole picture."

"What about the castration thing? Where does that fit in?"

He looked at me. "I don't know yet. Maybe the guy was a closet queen and couldn't stand the fact. All those biker types claim to be strictly heterosexual, but when I was working vice, I saw a lot of them take tenners from sick kids who melt at the sight of leather. Or maybe Hunter stole the guy's old lady from him at one time and the guy held a grudge. I don't know."

"If you're right, and it was one of the Warriors, he sure as hell didn't haul that body out of there on the back of a chopper. He had to have a car."

He nodded slowly. "We got some good tire prints where we think the guy pulled off the road to park. The ground was wet there, and the impressions came out pretty clear. We're checking them out now."

"What's your plan?"

The doors slid open, and we stepped off.

"To start pulling in all the Warriors for questioning and see what we come up with," he said, then glanced over my shoulder.

I turned to see what he was looking at. The man who had been accompanying Mrs. Muller was walking toward us. He looked to be in his late thirties, with prematurely thinning hair and a big-shouldered, heavy body that would have looked at home on the offensive front line of the L.A. Rams.

"Jacob Asch," Kleinst said as the other man came up, "my partner, Phil Cooley." He smiled suddenly and said: "We just call him Spade around the station house. It's no reflection on his race, you understand, just his personality. You remember Spade Cooley, don't you? He was that country and western fiddle player who stomped his wife to death a few years back, and made his kid watch the whole thing. That's what kind of a guy Phil here is. Sadistic."

Cooley listened to Kleinst's monologue with silent stoicism and then said: "Glad to meet you, Jake. Don't listen to this asshole's bullshit. He'll just keep dishing it out until your own eyes turn brown. I hear you were there when the girl got it."

"That's right."

"This sort of complicates matters now," he said, almost resentfully. "We thought we had it all worked out and then this bastard Hunter has to turn up dead. Well, those are the breaks. Hey listen, I don't like to interrupt anything, but I'd really like to talk to you alone, Harry."

"Sure," Kleinst said, then turned to me. "Excuse me, will you, Asch?"

"Sure," I said. "I've got to be going now anyway. Call me at home anytime if anything breaks."

CHAPTER TWENTY-FIVE

I left County Hospital and drove to Culver City. I wasn't suffering under the delusion that I could somehow accomplish something the police couldn't, but I felt as if I had to go through the motions at least, to trip myself out into believing that I was doing *something*. Or maybe it was just to delay that inevitable moment when I would go home and sit with a drink in front of the tube and see that bloody image that kept floating through my mind staring back at me from the set.

The lights inside Skip's Chop Shop were on as I cruised by. Through the open doors gunfire-bursts of a motor pierced the night quiet of the street. I couldn't see any bikes inside, so I parked and walked cautiously back to the doors and looked in.

Skip was alone, bent over the motor of a metal-flake green trike. The machine looked bizarre but somehow beautifully misshapen, with its two fat tires on the rear and its single skinny front tire raked far out in front of its bulky, squarish body. Skip had his finger on the throttle of the motor; he was revving it in rhythmical, deafening bursts. Then he looked up and saw me. He straightened up warily and the motor died down to an erratic purr.

"What do you want?"

"Just a little conversation."

His eyes were flat and depthless, as was his voice. "Yeah? About what?"

"Come on, Skip. You know what about. Gypsy."

He reached over and cut the ignition key on the trike. The motor sputtered and died. Then he walked casually over to his workbench and picked up a rag and began wiping his hands. "Listen, man, the pigs were already here once today. I told them I don't know where the fuck Gypsy is, and I meant it. So why don't you just putt on out of here and let me work?"

"I don't want to know where Gypsy is," I said. "I already know where he is. I just saw him, as a matter of fact."

"Yeah? Where?"

"In the morgue."

His mouth went slack. He stopped wiping his hands on the rag. "What the fuck are you talking about?"

"It's not that difficult to grasp, is it? Gypsy's dead."

He flung the rag down furiously and said: "Those fucking pigs. Those goddamn fascist bastards. It's a fucking plot to wipe us all out, man. They're just waiting for the chance. If some rich dude gets in trouble, all they do is kiss his ass and send him on his way, but the minute anything happens involving a Warrior, they blow him away—no questions asked. And nobody gives a shit. Nobody —nobody gives a shit in hell, it's, it's—"

His invective sputtered and died like the motor had. He stood there, glaring at me, the fury burning in his eyes.

"The cops didn't kill Gypsy," I said. "They found him this morning about five miles from Dirty Delbert's house, buried in a shallow grave."

He looked suddenly confused. "Who did it?"

"Nobody knows. I thought you might have some ideas on the subject."

"Me? How would I know?"

"Gypsy and Susan Gurney were killed in a rip-off. Whoever murdered them knew all about the extortion plot they'd cooked up and when the payoff was supposed to have been made. That means it was an accomplice or somebody who was a friend of theirs. Gypsy didn't have any friends except Warriors."

He poked a finger at me and said: "Are you trying to say that the Warriors had something to do with killing Gypsy? Is that what you're trying to say, man?"

"That's it."

"Well, you can forget it, man. We don't rip off our brothers."

"I know. You're a bunch of sweethearts. You only kill and maim strangers."

"We don't start hassles, but if some dude comes around and starts hassling us, he's gonna get his ass kicked. That's the way things are."

I ran a hand up along the side of my face, remembering how

things were. "Did Gypsy have any hassles going with anybody?"

"Like I said, man, Gypsy was a brother. We don't hassle with our brothers."

"Twenty-five thousand dollars could loosen a lot of brotherly bonds, don't you think?"

A look of surprise registered on his face. "Twenty-five thousand? What twenty-five thousand?"

"Didn't the cops tell you when they talked to you? Gypsy and the Gurney girl were working a fake kidnaping scheme to extort money from her parents. The ransom amount was twenty-five thousand bucks. Whoever killed them has it now."

He shook his head. "It don't matter if it was twenty-five million. Money's no good if you can't spend it. And if one of the Warriors ripped off Gypsy, he'd know he wouldn't be able to spend it."

"Why not?"

"Because he wouldn't be in the mood after being dragged from the back of a bike fifty miles across asphalt," he said seriously.

"Maybe you'd like to do some asking around," I suggested, "just to see if anybody you know has come into some money lately."

He leaned toward me and whispered hoarsely: "Maybe you'd like to get the fuck out of here."

"Sure. But if you find out anything, I wouldn't try any cross-country drags if I were you. The cops are going to be riding up your tailpipes from now on. Take it easy, Skip."

On my way home I stopped at a little health food restaurant on Santa Monica that I frequented occasionally and ordered a mixed green salad and a large glass of organic apple juice at the juice bar. My mind was unsettled by the direction things had taken during the last eight hours. There were too many pieces that didn't fit into the puzzle: the ferocity with which Susan Gurney and Hunter had been attacked, the motive for the Farnsworth murder, now that that was definitely tied in with the other two. I went through the events of the case slowly, trying to pick up a connecting thread. Then something began tugging persistently at the edge of my thoughts, something that had been there all along, but that I hadn't bothered to inspect closely because there had been no need. There was a need now.

CHAPTER TWENTY-SIX

The evening service was going full blast as I pulled up outside the commune gates and parked. A man's voice, trembling with emotion and amplified through electric guitar speakers, boomed from inside the main building. I walked to the building and went through the open door and slipped into an unoccupied seat toward the rear. The room was about two-thirds full, and nobody seemed to notice me come in. Their collective attention was focused on the wild, pacing figure on the stage.

It was Sievers, but Sievers transformed. He had removed the microphone from its stand and was holding the trailing cord with his other hand. He was stalking the audience, his eyes glowing like two red-hot rivets, his face glistening sweat. He was alive with something, the Holy Spirit or charisma or whatever anybody wanted to call it, it was undeniably there—the Power—and he was using it to work the audience.

"Does anyone here doubt that the Judgment is upon us?" he was saying.

He stopped dead center on the stage and looked down at the front rows. "Because all any of you has to do is look around at the state of the world to see the truth. We are told that science is the cure-all to man's problems, but look at the problems this false god has created. I say to you that science is the tool of Satan to take man's mind off the truth. Satan is the prince of education and culture and the arts, and they, like him, are doomed."

"Amen!"

"Satan is the master magician and that is his big trick—TO KEEP YOUR MINDS OCCUPIED WHILE HE STEALS YOUR SOULS. He will give you dope and sex and money, but those things won't get you high. All they'll do is put you to sleep."

"Praise the Lord!"

171

"Right on, brother!"

"That lid you bought, that's just to make you forget, so you'll fall. Satan wants company when he is cast into the abyss." His eyes swept the front row and lighted on a black-haired girl sitting near the aisle. His voice dropped into a low, quivering lament, and he said: "How about you, sister? Are you going to go with him?"

The girl broke into a wail and started to sob, then stood up and raised her hands over her head and stumbled blindly toward the stage. When she reached the foot of the stage, her legs gave way and she dropped to her knees, still sobbing.

Sievers closed his eyes dramatically and raised his face toward the ceiling and thrust his hands out over the girl. "Open up your life and accept Jesus into your heart. Open up the dikes and let the Holy Spirit flood into you and BE SAVED!"

The girl suddenly gagged, and a strange, gurgling sound issued from her throat. Her back began swaying as if the floor were tilting underneath her. Then her back arched convulsively and her neck bent backwards. She toppled to the floor and lay there twitching violently. Another girl from the front row stood up and screamed and fell, writhing on the floor. Pretty soon half the front row was on the floor while the rest of the congregation left their seats and formed a semicircle around the blessed quiverers, going through their vowels with their hands raised to heaven.

After about ten minutes, the excitement died down. The possessed had regained control of themselves and resumed their seats. Sievers was declaring it a "miracle of God" that so many souls had been delivered to Christ tonight, and apparently sensing that anything else would be anticlimactic, he ended the sermon with a prayer and stepped down off the stage.

Everybody stood up and began leaving their seats. I went down the aisle, excusing my way through the crowd, trying to get to Sievers. He was up front, talking to his newfound converts, consolidating his wins. I was only about ten feet away when a pair of hands clamped tightly onto each of my arms, halting me in my tracks. It was Isaiah and the black militant, Joshua.

"Where do you think you're going?" Isaiah sneered.

"I've got to talk to Sievers. It's important."

"You're not talking to anybody. You're going out."

They turned me around and started pulling me toward the

door. I planted my feet and wrenched my arms free and took a quick step back so that I was behind them.

They both whirled around and I held up a hand in warning. "Ex-Green Beret or no ex-Green Beret, you put your goddamn hands on me again, 'Brother Isaiah,' and somebody's going to bleed. And some of your new converts may have a relapse at the sight of blood."

His face flushed anger, and he dropped into a fighting crouch and started toward me. "I've been waiting for this for a long time. . . ."

I took another step back and got set. I knew it would be no contest, that I was going to get butchered, but I wanted to get in one good punch before it was all over. He came with his hands loose and confident and I dug my toes in and cocked my right fist back, waiting for him to make his move, but then Sievers came pushing through the crowd that had instantly formed around us, and Isaiah straightened up.

"What's going on?" Sievers demanded. He saw me and his eyes narrowed savagely. "What are you doing here? I thought I made it clear you weren't welcome here."

"You did. But I've got to talk to you."

"We have nothing to talk about. We're all talked out."

"Maybe we *were*, but a lot of things have happened since then. You must have heard about the girl. They just found her boyfriend buried in a shallow grave not far from the house where she was killed. The cops have also matched up the bullets taken from Susan Gurney's body with the ones that killed Farnsworth. That makes three murders, Sievers, and the person who committed them is still running around loose. You want to talk to me or you want to wait until it's four?"

He looked around uneasily, obviously distressed by what impact all this might have on his young followers, and said quickly: "All right. We can talk outside."

"Not with this goon," I said, pointing at Isaiah. "Alone."

Isaiah took a step toward me. "Why you—"

"That's enough," Sievers said sharply. The reproval checked Isaiah's forward motion. Sievers watched him, making sure it was permanently checked, then turned to me. "Okay. Let's go outside."

The circle of bodies broke before us and we walked to the door

173

and stepped outside. Stars flecked the black night sky and a crescent moon hovered close to the mountains. Just outside the door, Sievers stopped and turned. "All right, Asch, now what's this all about?"

"I have a theory about who killed Susan Gurney. I'm hoping you can confirm it for me."

"Me?" he exclaimed. "How would I know who killed the girl?"

"I think she told you."

"I don't understand. How could she tell me who killed her?"

"When I first came to see you about the girl, you told me that she had laid out her sinful past to you. When I asked you to elaborate, you refused. I think it was her past, or at least part of it, that caught up with her at that house the other night. I think Larry Farnsworth was killed because Susan told him her deep dark secrets, too. Except he tried to make a little extra cash off them and got blown away because of it."

"You don't think—" he started, then cut himself off.

"Think what?"

He stared off at the moon silently, gathering his thoughts.

"Look, Sievers, the cops will get it all anyway. Whatever Susan told you isn't covered by any legal rules of confidentiality. You're not a priest. You can't withhold information in a homicide case."

"I've never withheld information," he snapped. "If I'd been aware I was in possession of any pertinent information, I would have gladly volunteered it. All the news reports I've heard said that the police were looking for the boyfriend. It sounded as if they had it all tied up. As far as I could see, there could be no point in digging into the girl's past sins. She is already paying for them in Hell."

"There's reason now. What did she tell you? It involved Haynes, didn't it?"

He sighed. "Yes. She confessed she had been living in abomination with him since she was fourteen."

"You mean, she was having sexual relations with him."

"Yes."

Even though it had all come together for me over an hour ago, or at least an inkling of it, I felt an exhilaration, a great feeling of release, having it confirmed.

Sievers looked at me searchingly and asked: "Is that who you think killed her? Haynes?"

"That's going to be for the police to decide," I said, deliberately hedging the question. "I think that was the reason she was killed, though. Does Haynes know you know what was going on?"

"Not unless she told him. I certainly didn't."

"Did she say anything else about Haynes to you, except about the affair she was having with him?"

"She warned me he would probably try to take her out of here if he ever found out she was here. That was why she said it was important that her parents never found out she was here. She said he thought he was in love with her and wanted her to run away with him. But she wouldn't do it. She was thoroughly disgusted at the evil life she had been leading and wanted to repent. It was a stupid mistake of hers using that credit card. I don't know how she could have been so blind."

I nodded. The moon was making its ascent into the night sky now, a cold, pale reminder of death. "I'm going to call the sheriff in L.A. I'll probably be coming back with them in a little while. They'll want to talk to you about this."

He nodded. Inside the building the disciples had started into the first chorus of "Oh Happy Day." Sievers seemed oblivious to the raucous voices that poured through the open doors. He shook his head thoughtfully and stared off over the tops of the mountains. "You know, when she poured it all out to me, I could see it was going to be a pitched battle with Lucifer for her soul. I knew it would be a struggle, but I was sure I could win and save her soul from eternal damnation. But Satan had too strong a grip on her."

"You sound as if you're more disturbed by the fact of your own personal failure than with her damnation."

"The loss of every soul to Satan is a cause of grievance to me," he said pontifically. "But the Judgment is too close to dwell on individual losses. At this late date, only numbers count, how many will be saved to reap the coming Kingdom of God."

"I think you actually believe all that shit."

"Of course I believe it."

"Well, it's comforting to know that it won't be keeping you up at night worrying about me burning in Hell. I wouldn't want to be burdened with that responsibility."

"I can assure you it won't. But I *will* pray for you, that you may find the Way before it is too late for you."

"Don't bother," I snapped, seething from the pitying tone of his voice.

He turned and went back through the doorway.

I stood outside the door for a few minutes, listening to the ecstatic voices of the singers piercing the night, then walked briskly to my car, feeling somehow strangely violated.

CHAPTER TWENTY-SEVEN

It was after one when I pulled up in front of the house and parked. The floodlights outside were on, bathing the statues in a cold blue light. I killed my own lights and waited in the dark.

About ten minutes later three sets of headlights came up the hill and pulled up behind me and I opened the door and stepped out. The doors of the unmarked Plymouth directly behind me flew open and Kleinst and Cooley stepped out.

Kleinst came over to me. "Okay now, you remember what I told you. You go in last and keep your mouth shut."

"Right," I said. "And listen, I really appreciate you letting me be in on the bust—"

"Just remember what I told you," he said, and turned back toward the others coming up to us. Besides Cooley, there were four others whom I didn't recognize. Two of them were carrying sawed-off, pump-action 12 gauges.

"Zelazny," Kleinst said to two of them, "you and Murphy go around the back and watch the rear doors. There's a kitchen door and a sliding glass door leading from the pool to the living room and another sliding glass door leading into one of the bedrooms. That right, Asch?"

I nodded.

"Roberts, you and Triolo stay down here and watch the front. And none of you make a move unless you hear it from me. This asshole's got money, and I don't want his attorney screaming later in court about police brutality and constitutional rights. Got it?"

They nodded and the two with the 12 gauges started up the hill toward the back. Kleinst, Cooley, and I waited until they were at the fence before we started up.

At the door, Kleinst and Cooley unbuttoned their sports jackets, and Kleinst pushed the doorbell and stood back.

Nothing happened when Kleinst rang the bell, so he pushed it again. After a few more minutes there was a scuffling noise behind the door, and it was pulled open. Haynes was standing there blinking out at us with bloodshot eyes. He was a mess. The sport shirt he was wearing looked as if he had been sleeping in it. His face was covered with a coarse gray stubble that glistened in the overhead porch light.

"Sorry to bother you so late, Mr. Haynes," Kleinst said apologetically, "but something has come up that we need to talk to you about. May we come in?"

Haynes peered at us obtusely, then shook his head, as if to clear his thoughts. "Wha—what's all this about? Can't it wait until morning?" His vision focused on me then, and his mouth tightened into an angry pink scar. "What the hell is *he* doing here?"

"Asch is one of the reasons we're here," Kleinst said honestly. "We've made a breakthrough in your daughter's case—"

He looked at us uneasily. "Breakthrough? What breakthrough?"

"That's what we want to talk to you about."

"That son of a bitch isn't setting foot in my house," Haynes snarled. "He's the one responsible for my Susie's death."

It was a good act. I was beginning to think he almost had himself believing it.

"I know," Kleinst said, humoring him. "But it might be easier with him here to clear up a few points."

Haynes scowled at me belligerently. I knew that if he protested again about my presence, even weakly, Kleinst would tell me to go back to the car, and that would be that. But he didn't. After a brief hesitation, he grudgingly pulled open the door and stood back.

We stepped inside, and he closed the door, telling us to go into the living room. He bumped his shoulder rounding the corner into the living room. Kleinst and Cooley kept on his heels, watching him closely. He went into the room and sat down heavily in one of the chairs.

I looked out the sliding glass door to the pool, but all I could see was our four ghostly reflections in the glass. The other plainclothesmen were not visible.

Haynes looked up at us with annoyance. "Okay, so what's all this about?"

Kleinst moved around so that he was standing a few feet away from Haynes' chair. Cooley had placed himself strategically in a direct line with the hallway.

"We've turned up an important witness in your stepdaughter's case."

"Witness? What witness?"

"Aaron Sievers."

"That religious shyster? He's involved in Susan's murder?"

"No. But Susan told him the same thing she told Farnsworth. The same little matter Farnsworth was using to blackmail you."

The color drained from Haynes' face. He looked as if he were going to pass out. He must have realized what he looked like, because he blinked twice and knitted his eyebrows, trying to look confused. "What are you talking about?"

"You're under arrest for the murder of your stepdaughter, that's what I'm talking about," Kleinst said coldly.

Haynes tried to say something, but Kleinst held up a hand and cut him off. "Before you say anything, I have to read you your rights." He pulled out a notebook and began reading wearily. "You have the right to remain silent. You do not have to answer any questions. If you do answer questions, your answers may be used in evidence against you. You have the right to legal counsel. If you cannot afford an attorney, the state will appoint one for you at your request without any expense on your part. Do you understand your rights as I have explained them to you?"

I became aware of another presence in the room and turned to see Cynthia Haynes standing in the entrance to the hallway. Her hair was disheveled from sleep, and she was clutching her bathrobe tightly at her throat. She looked pale, almost chalk white. "What's going on here? Robert, what is this?"

"Just a minute, please," Kleinst said sharply, seemingly irritated by the interruption. "Do you understand your rights as I have explained them to you?"

Haynes swallowed hard and licked his lips. "Yes," he said weakly.

"Won't somebody please tell me what's going on?" Mrs. Haynes repeated.

"They say I killed Susan," Haynes told her.

"What?!" she thundered angrily. "This is absurd. You can't come charging into this house in the middle of the night like some

179

gestapo storm troopers, throwing slanderous accusations around like that. I'll have your badge for this, sergeant—"

"I'm sorry about the time, Mrs. Haynes, but we didn't pick it."

She wheeled on me and pinned me with a venomous stare. "This must be *his* doing. What ridiculous story did he tell you?"

"It's not so ridiculous," Kleinst said. "As a matter of fact, it makes a lot of sense."

"What sense? What are you talking about?"

"Your husband had been carrying on an illicit affair with your daughter for the past four years, in case you don't know. She told several people about it. Larry Farnsworth was one. It must have come out while he was deprogramming her, and then he tried to use it to work a little blackmail scheme against your husband by threatening to tell Eric Gurney what he knew. But it backfired, and he got murdered instead. Susan also told Aaron Sievers about it. She had a big load of guilt to dump when she joined the Word of God, and she dumped it all on him."

"How do you know all this?" she asked accusingly.

"Sievers confirmed it all for us."

"What's his word worth? What's any of this so-called evidence worth?" She threw a sharp glance at me. "The testimony of a religious charlatan who makes his money by fleecing credulous teenagers and the word of a two-bit private detective who's trying to save his own professional reputation by throwing out a lot of wild accusations, hoping some of them will stick."

"We've got more than accusations," Kleinst said deliberately. "Even without Asch giving us the tip, we would have had it all nailed down in a couple of days anyway. Once we'd made the identification of the tire tracks—"

"What tire tracks?" Haynes said, his eyes widening.

"The tire tracks at John Hunter's gravesite. Because of Asch's tip, we were able to get an identification of them right away, but we would have had it all worked out in a day or so anyway. There aren't very many cars that stock Dunlop tires. They're only on foreign cars. Especially that size."

"That doesn't prove anything. My car isn't the only one in the city with Dunlop tires on it."

"It's probably the only one that belongs to someone who had a motive and the opportunity for murder. We checked out your car on the way up. I see you washed it since yesterday."

"That's right," Haynes said with a hollow defiance. The artery on the right side of his temple was beginning to pulse violently. "Can't I wash my own car when it gets dirty?"

"Sure," Kleinst said casually. "What was it dirty from?"

"From the road." His voice had acquired an assertive edge, as if he were trying to rally all of his inner forces for one final defense. "Cars *do* get dirty, you know."

Kleinst nodded. "Especially if you haul bleeding bodies around in them." He paused and stared at Haynes, whose grip had tightened on the arms of his chair. "You know, you couldn't have gotten it all, Haynes. The lab boys even amaze me when they really go to work. A little mud sample from the inside of a wheel well, part of a bloodstain, a strand of hair. You know, you can actually build an entire case around one little tiny strand of hair? Did you know that, Haynes? It may not seem like much to base a case on, but when you get right down to it, circumstantial evidence is probably the most reliable and strongest kind of evidence to insure a conviction. Witnesses can lie or see things that aren't there, but circumstantial evidence doesn't lie."

Kleinst's soft-voiced lecture on the finer points of homicide detection was starting to have its effect on Haynes. His eyes darted around the room, looking for escape, and his knuckles were turning white on the arms of the chair.

"It's no good, Haynes," Kleinst said in an almost paternal tone. "The guilt is written all over your face. Look at yourself. You're sweating. Your mouth is dry. Why don't you tell us about it and get it off your chest? It must be eating you up inside."

All the color had drained from Haynes' face now. His lips moved, groping for words, but no sound came out.

"We know you didn't mean to do it," Kleinst went on. "We know it was just one of those things that happened. For your own sanity, why don't you let it go? We know how you felt about the girl—"

Haynes buried his face in his hands and said: "No you don't. You couldn't. Nobody could. I—I. . . ."

Cynthia had moved into the room silently, her eyes glued to the figure of her husband. She sat down on the edge of the chair with her mouth open slightly, her hands balled into bloodless fists.

Kleinst put his hand on Haynes' shoulder and patted it sympathetically.

Haynes looked up pleadingly into Kleinst's falsely paternal eyes. "I—I didn't mean to kill her. I only took the gun because I thought she might be in trouble and need me. I couldn't believe that she'd do that to me, what Asch said. But when I heard them talking—"

"Susan and Asch?"

He nodded and swallowed. "I was outside the window. I heard her talking about how she was planning to run away with that, that animal, and I, I don't know, I just went crazy. She couldn't treat me like that. She was nothing but a little whore, she, she—"

His voice broke off, and he seemed to be trying to catch his breath. Kleinst said: "Then you went into the house—"

"I went around to the front door and waited there. I couldn't let Asch get away with that money, don't you see, it was my ticket out of this—"

His eyes rolled around, and he went on. "I hit him with the gun when he came through the door. Then I went inside. She was standing there in the middle of the room. I told her I had the money now and that we could take it and leave together, go away somewhere. She just laughed. Then she started calling me names."

His words were racing now, trying to keep up with his thoughts. "That little whore was calling *me* names. I had to make her shut up. I hit her with the gun, and she fell back on the couch, and I hit her again and again." His eyes were wide, as if he were watching a motion picture that was being run inside of his head.

"And then what?" Kleinst leaned forward, prompting him.

He closed his eyes. "I, I shot her."

"How many times?"

"I don't remember."

"Then what happened?"

"I heard a groan . . . in the kitchen . . . and I went in there and saw Hunter on the floor. His face was bleeding, and I kicked him and told him to get up, and he saw the gun and got scared and asked where Susan was. I told him to shut up and go into the living room. He saw her and then he turned around and tried to grab the gun, and I shot him."

He was calm now. A film of perspiration stood out on his chalky face.

"And after you'd done it, you thought that if you took Hunter's body and buried it, we'd think he'd killed Susan and taken the money."

"Hhmm?" he asked, staring glassily into space. He was starting to go into a mild shock; his mind was drifting. "Yes. No. I mean, I guess so. I don't remember, really. All I remember is finding a shovel in the house and wrapping up his body and then, and then, I, I was driving home on the freeway, and the body wasn't in the car anymore. Just the blood. There was blood everywhere in the back seat. And the lights from the cars were in my eyes . . . I. . . ."

"And Farnsworth—you killed him, too, right?"

He held out his hands in a pleading gesture and said: "He was going to tell Eric about us. He said he wanted money. I knew it would never end and that I couldn't keep it up, not with *her* leaning over my shoulder every time I wrote a check, wanting to know what it was for. If Eric had found out, it would have been over, don't you see? He would have had Susie taken away from me, and I couldn't let that happen. . . ."

Cynthia was staring at her husband, her face white. "My God. I had no idea—"

Haynes' head jerked toward her violently. "Maybe you didn't want to admit it to yourself, but you knew. You frigid bitch. You're the one who did this to me. You put us together every chance you could. You made sure we had plenty of opportunities."

Her eyes were wide in fright. She shook her head weakly.

"You'd always get a headache conveniently and go to bed and leave us alone to watch television together. You made sure we had plenty of privacy. You used your own daughter to take the heat off yourself so you wouldn't have to have your precious body defiled—"

"No, it's a lie," she said, but the resolution was gone from her voice. She looked toward me with pleading eyes. "Mr. Asch, you know that's not true. She was my daughter. I wouldn't do something like that to my own daughter."

I stared at her without saying anything. She shook her head from side to side, then buried her face in her hands.

I turned back to Haynes. "I have a question, Haynes. Why didn't you kill me, too?"

He looked over at me, his face an expressionless mask. "I didn't have any bullets left."

The flat, toneless quality of his voice sent a numbing chill through me. Suddenly I felt drained and tired and very, very old. The other voices in the room grew faint, as if they were speaking from the bottom of a deep well. For a split second, I was totally alone, touching something dark and cold. Then they came back again, and I heard Kleinst saying: "You want to stand up, Mr. Haynes?"

Haynes stood up mechanically and Kleinst pulled his arms behind him and snapped on the cuffs, and they started toward the door.

I followed. As I passed Mrs. Haynes she reached out and clutched the sleeve of my coat. Her eyes were dark, depthless prayers. "I didn't know," she said weakly. "I really didn't."

I took her wrist gently from my arm, then turned without speaking and went toward the door.